1990

PALABRA SUR

Cecilia Vicuña, *Series Editor*

THE CARDBOARD HOUSE

by

MARTÍN ADÁN

Translated & with an Introduction by

KATHERINE SILVER

A PALABRA SUR BOOK

GRAYWOLF PRESS

A Palabra Sur Book. *Palabra Sur* is a series of translations of significant Latin American works. The series was conceived and is edited by Cecilia Vicuña; the series advisory board includes Suzanne Jill Levine, Magda Bogin, Gregory Rabassa, and Eliot Weinberger.

Publication of this volume is made possible in part by grants from the National Endowment for the Arts, the Unity Avenue Foundation, the Minnesota State Arts Board, and the New York Council on the Arts. Graywolf Press is the recipient of a McKnight Foundation Award administered by the Minnesota State Arts Board and receives generous contributions from corporations, foundations, and individuals. Graywolf Press is a member agency of United Arts, Saint Paul. Translation of this book was supported by a National Endowment for the Arts Fellowship Grant.

Published by GRAYWOLF PRESS
2402 University Avenue, Suite 203
Saint Paul, Minnesota 55114

9 8 7 6 5 4 3 2
First Printing, 1990

Library of Congress Cataloging-in-Publication Data

Adán, Martín, 1908-
[Casa de cartón. English]
The cardboard house / by Martín Adán ; translated and
with an introduction by Katherine Silver.
p.   cm. – (A Palabra sur book)
Translation of: La casa de cartón.
ISBN 1-55597-129-6 : $17.95X
I. Title.   II. Series: Palabra Sur.
PQ8497.F83C313   1990
863–dc20   90-31855

THE CLIFFS overlooking the Pacific Ocean are only a ten-minute bus ride away from the dirty, crowded, ashen-colored streets of downtown Lima. *Beyond the city: the clear tender chasm of the sea.* Walking south on the promenade that winds along the edge of these cliffs, you soon reach *the last stretch on the way to Chorrillos, zigzagging, seascape in relief, chiseled with a knife, a sailor's toy.* On the way, you pass by Mario Vargas Llosa's walled mansion. From the large picture windows of his third-floor studio, he can see the *sea that is never pale green, but has zones that are grey, colorless, lined with the tracks of ducks; full of minute coasts and feeble backgrounds.* Scattered here and there along Barranco's *promenade with ancient gardens of fragile roses and dirty and dwarfed palm trees . . . with one hour of quietude: six o'clock in the afternoon . . .* are the homes of other well-known artists and intellectuals, modern architectural experiments, decaying villas, a sudden hovel.

Continuing in the same direction, you soon reach a plaza: there is a pond, strangely shaped trees with bright pink flowers, and a plaster of Paris Venus *with a bird perched on its head.* The avenues leading out from the plaza are lined with jacaranda trees *that produce many purple flowers . . . a solemn, old-fashioned, confidential, expressive, gaudy, mindful, family tree.* A newspaper vendor stands on one corner, and his *Cronica and Comercio newspapers are blown about until the cart threatens to roll backwards.* On another street corner stands an Indian woman *with her hard, shiny, damp head of hair – a mud carving . . .* selling her single cigarettes and chewing gum.

This is the setting – geographically – of *The Cardboard House.* To find it in time, we must turn back to the first few decades of the twentieth century when Martín Adán, née Rafael de la Fuente Benavides, spent his summer vacations here with his family. Then an exclusive seaside resort, it is now just another of Lima's many decaying and slovenly neighborhoods.

When Adán began composing *The Cardboard House* at the age of eighteen, Barranco for him was also fragments of memory, imagination, sensations, nostalgic yearnings. The resort, as he had known it, and his place in it, had ceased to exist. His family, aristocratic but in full economic decadence, had sold their Barranco chalet some years before to pay off debts. With the money that was left over, they purchased a Ford automobile so that Rafael's mother and aunts could "go to church in style." (Mirko Lauer, *Los Exilios Interiores*)

Biographical information about Martín Adán is sparse and

anecdotal. He was born in Lima in 1908. By the time he was a young adult, he had lost every member of his immediate family: his younger brother died when they were children, then his father, his mother, and finally the aunt and uncle under whose care he had been placed. He attended the German High School, where many of his classmates and teachers were or would become leading figures in Peru's artistic and intellectual life.

When *The Cardboard House* was published in 1928, it was received with high critical acclaim. Adán was hailed as a great innovator of Peruvian literature and the most promising young writer of his generation. For a while he moved in Lima's literary circles and marginally participated in the political and cultural debates that raged at that time.

Soon thereafter, the traces of his life fade into an alcoholic haze. There are anecdotes about the coffee houses he visited, the odd scrapes of napkins on which he wrote his poetry, and his increasing isolation, an isolation that became absolute when he committed himself to a "house of rest," less euphemistically called a psychiatric hospital. There he remained until 1985, when his physical condition necessitated his removal to a different kind of hospital. He died that same year.

During his almost forty years of self-imposed confinement, he jealously guarded his solitude, shunning all public attention and only allowing visits from his editor, Juan Mejía Baca, and a few close friends. During one of the only interviews he ever granted – and this after the interviewer had spent years soliciting a meeting that Adán cut short after a few questions – he said he wrote *The Cardboard House* to practice the rules his grammar professor, Emilio Huidobro, had given him.

The Cardboard House is the only piece of prose Martín Adán ever completed. Some six or seven volumes of poetry were published during his lifetime and this due largely to the painstaking and devoted labor of Mejía Baca, who collected the bits and pieces of paper Adán left strewn along his path. Though he never quite lived up to the expectations created by the brilliance of *The Cardboard House,* he is still commonly referred to as one of the greatest Latin American poets of all time.

I am not wholly convinced of my own humanity: I do not wish to be like others. I do not want to be happy with permission of the police.

The world is insufficient for me.

The Peruvian writer and critic, Luis Loayza, called *The Cardboard House* "a long prose poem that always returns to the same place, to a particular memory." According to Mario Vargas Llosa, Adán wanted only to "transmit the impressions, sensations, and emotions that this neighborhood of nine thousand souls meant for him in his childhood and youth." Vargas Llosa also considered it, "a profoundly realistic book . . . essential realism . . . not a reproduction of the exterior reality, but rather a poetic, sensual, intuitive, nonrational testimony of that reality."

The Cardboard House is composed of a series of fragments or scenes. Each fragment, and even each image within each fragment, is a world unto itself, vibrating through Adán's power of evocation only at the moment it is being read, without referring necessarily to that which comes before or after. Most critics have given up looking for any thematic or narrative development, and the only human beings that could possibly qualify as characters are the narrator himself and his friend, alter ego, and rival, Ramon.

The Cardboard House notably distinguishes itself from most other Latin American literature of that era through its profound vein of irony and humor. Adán borrows – from Proust, from

Joyce, from Góngora – but he laughs at himself for doing so, as he laughs at his nation for that *native and premature desire that Europe will make of us men*. He makes no bones about who he is: a provincial boy in a semicolonial world who experiences the modern world as it is exported to him. "Gringos" appear right next to "Indians." They look, smell, talk, and act differently. *This one was an Englishman who fished with a reed . . . A Poet? Nothing of the sort: a travel agent from Dawson and Brothers LTD . . . Or Miss Annie Doll . . . Synthetic milk, canned meat, hard liquor . . . a red, long, sinewy, mobile thing that carries a Kodak over its shoulder and asks questions that are wise, useless, and senseless.*

Though subtle and lyrical, this narrative is as profoundly subversive now as it was when it was written. Adán's uncompromising poetic vision and the trueness and purity of his voice constitute a heroic act against cultural colonialism: a reclamation of the word and the world for his, or their, own use.

The Cardboard House presents unique difficulties and exhilarating challenges to the translator. I found myself working image by image rather than by word or sentence or paragraph. I attempted, as I hope the reader shall too, to remain with Adán at each precise instant, to savor each sight, smell, or flight of fancy his language evokes. I consciously resisted the temptation to explain and to simplify. Whenever possible without betraying Adán's purity, his youthful audacity, I attempted to unveil the mystery, shorten the spacial and temporal, as well as linguistic distances that separate Adán from his contemporary readers in English. I can only hope that my interpretation has not diminished the brilliance of this small, unique gem, this extraordinary flash of genius from the seacoast of the south.

KATHERINE SILVER

NOTE: All italics are quotes from my translation of *The Cardboard House.*

BIBLIOGRAPHY

Chumbiauca, Oswaldo, "Martín Adán rompe el silencio." *Revista Poesía,* #60–61, Vol. XI, No. 1–2, March–June, 1984.

Lauer, Mirko. *Los exilios interiores.* Lima, Hueso Humero Ediciones, 1983.

Vargas Llosa, Mario "Hombres, libros, ideas. La Casa de cartón." *Cultura Peruana,* #19, November, 1959.

· THE CARDBOARD HOUSE ·

WINTER in Barranco has already begun; a peculiar, daft, and fragile winter that just may cleave the sky and let a tip of summer peek through. The mist of this small winter, affairs of the soul, puffs of sea breeze, the drizzle of a boat trip from one pier to another, the sonorous flutter of rushing laysisters, opaque sounds of mass, winter newly arrived. . . . Now, off to school with cold hands. Breakfast is a warm ball in the stomach, the hardness of the dining room chair on the buttocks, and the solemn desire in the entire body not to go to school. The frond of a palm tree hovers over a house: flabellate, gently somber, pure, pink, glistening. And now you whistle with the streetcar, boy with closed eyes. You do not understand how one can possibly go to school so early in the morning, especially with promenades and the sea below. But, as you walk down the street that traverses almost the entire city, you smell the perfume of distant vegetables in nearby gardens. You think of the lush, wet fields: almost urban behind you; limitless in front of you, between the ash and elder trees, towards the bluish sierra. Barely the outline of the first foothills, the mountains' brow. . . . And now you pass through the fields surrounded by muffled beehive sounds of fleeting friction over rails and a flourish of athletic yet urban gymnastics. Now the sun grinds to golden a mountain peak and an ancient burial mound, a yellow knoll like the sun itself. And you do not want it to be summer, but rather winter vacation, tiny and weak, with no school and no heat.

B EYOND the fields: the mountains; before the fields: the creek lined with alder trees and women washing clothes and children, all the same color of indifferent dirt. It is two o'clock in the afternoon. The sun struggles to free its rays from the branches into which it has fallen captive. The sun: a rare, hard, golden, lanky coleopteran. Father parish priest doffs his shovel hat, tilts his head, eleven reflections off a tall silk hat, a top hat – eleven reflections that converge overhead in a round, convex light. Beyond the city: the clear, tender chasm of the sea. The sea can be seen from above, at the risk of falling from the heights. The cliffs have wrinkles and spotless smooth patches and are livid and jaundiced on their geologic – academic – faces. There, in miniature, are the four ages of the world, the four dimensions of all things, the four cardinal points, everything, everything. One old man ... Two old men ... Three old men ... Three Pierola supporters. Three hours of sunshine must be wrested from the night. Their clothes are large, hanging loosely off their bodies. The smooth cloth is squared, trihedral, falls, grows taut – the cloth: empty within. The bones creak in time with the timed gestures, with the rhythmic stretching of hands to the sky along the horizon – the plane that intersects that of the sea to form angle X, Beginning Geometry, last chapter (first semester) – the sky where Pierola most likely is. The old men's whiskers slice into fine strips like expensive jelly the sea breeze and infuse it with the scent of guava trees, tobacco from Tumbes, herb-scented handkerchiefs, Peruvian cough syrups. A six-colored flag, wafted gently by a high wind not felt from below, suggests the flanks of a Spanish dancer. The Consulate General of Tomesia – a country created by Giraudoux out of a Hungarian plain, two Lima millionaires, several English trees, and the tone of an embroidered Chinese sky. Tomesia: never far from its Consulate General. The ice cream vendor's cart passes behind an old nag dangling its rough, blanched tongue. The poor beast would love to eat the ices in the hidden bucket; elegant and opaque lucuma-flavored ices, just barely chilled; ice creams, ample and pretty like a youthful portrait of mother sitting beside father; pine-apple-flavored ices that belong to red carnations; light and unfamiliar orange-flavored ices. How this cart does sound! The poor thing tears its soul out on the stones. And it would not alter its course for anything in the world, its straight course beyond the walls of the dead-end street, straight into imbecility. Oh little cart, cross over this lawn kept supple for you by the water of the fountain. Between things there exist bonds of mutual aid hampered by man. The rumble of the cart's wheels on the paving stones gladdens the sad waters of the fountain. The mestizo – his cheeks the color of blood-soaked earth and his nose sprinkled with tiny, round drops of sweat – the mestizo carter does not allow the cart to roll over the lawn of that meager garden. The old men make comments: "It's cold. Yesterday? ... A beautiful day! Whatever you say, Menganez ... "

I N   T H E morning, at the cutting edge of dawn, from the casement windows of the towers and in the awkward flight of frightened birds and the soggy ringing of bells, the old lay-sisters descend through the fog to their witches' sabbath of trees and lampposts. Black bulks sway to and fro, an infinity of arms, clawed hands, mumbled watchwords. . . . And the city is an oleograph we contemplate, sunken under water: the waves carry things away and alter the orientation of the planes. Lay-sisters who smell of sun and dew, of the dampness of towels left lying behind the bathtub, of elixirs, of eyewash, of the devil, of sponges: that dry, hollow smell of a soapy, worn, discolored pumice stone ... Lay-sisters who smell of dirty clothes, stars, cat fur, lamp oil, sperm ... Lay-sisters who smell of weeds, darkness, the litany, flowers for the dead ... Limpid gowns, metallic slippers ... The rosary is carried against the breast and makes no sound. At noon the sun shines down liquid and leaden like a yellow splash of water during carnival time of old. The streetcars carry their cargo of hats. Ah, the wind, such joy in this sea of gravity! The *Cronica* and *Comercio* newspapers are blown about until the cart threatens to roll backwards into an oblique flight over rails and lampposts. A tollbooth jumps to safety. The cart is halted by the station office, like a rolling ball in the classroom by the teacher.

T HE AFTERNOON, for the last time. Now we are crossing the Plazuela de San Francisco accompanied by the clipped tolling of bells for novena. A wall that blocks the towers – beautifully ugly – has, on the other hand, three picture windows of sleepy blue crystal illuminated by glimpses of the facing sky. This street leads to the sea: a sea no one sees, just like in the major ports. It is not today that we cross the Plazuela de San Francisco; we did it yesterday, while you were telling me how the twilight hurt your eyes. You were chewing on a leaf of a hedge bush and rubbing the fingernails of one hand against those of the other. I feared you would confide in me – always with so much sincerity — so, to prevent you from speaking, I recalled out loud a distant afternoon that was a prank, a huge fried egg, an embossed sun of brilliant gold almost peripheral to the rugged and aqueous porcelain sky, a nutritive afternoon that stained gluttonous poets from their foreheads to their noses with sunset hues. Movie houses bleat in their dark and filthy cribs. A turkey vulture, at the top of a flagpole, is a baby turkey — arched blackness and gray beak. An old woman walked aimlessly along the promenade, then dramatically took off to who knows where. An automobile turned on its headlight, revealing a cone of drizzle. We felt the cold on our eyelids. Yesterday . . . Bass Street now consoles us with its shadowy alcoves, its pharmaceutical smells of eucalyptus, its medicinal words, its rows of consumptive trees. And there is nobody who isn't you or I.

RAMON put on his glasses, and his face and legs looked more Negroid than ever. He said yes and filled his pockets with his hands. A bright star quivered in the sky; another star trembled closer by. The sky was night blue, with strands of day, with threads of day, feminine, seamstral. The scissors of wind sounded as in a poultry shop, and it was difficult to know if one's own hair or the Chinese silk of the sky was being cut. With humility Ramon divested himself of hope, the way he would have divested himself of his hat. Life, and he who was beginning to live ... One must resign oneself, he said, quoting Schopenhauer, then breathed deeply, as if asleep. I preferred Kempis to

Schopenhauer. Nietzsche was a farce. Ramon had not read Nietzsche, but he had heard of Superman. He knew that Superman was an alias of Firpo. He was beginning to live. . . . Obligatory military service . . . A possible war . . . Children, inevitable . . . Old age . . . The daily grind . . . I delicately whispered to him words of consolation, but I failed to console him; he hunched his shoulders and knit his brow; he rested his elbows on his knees; he was a failure. At sixteen years old! . . . Oh, to think what had befallen him! He almost cried; a spinster on a bicycle prevented him. A bright star crackled in the sky; another one was extinguished closer by. A mongrel and transient dog watched us walking, looking back. I spelled out the words for him with my fingers: "It's nothing. Don't be a pest." We went to Lima. The automobile tires sparked along the sticky asphalt; a flash of golden satin at the end of each block; the telephone posts mirrored one another perfectly; the pigeons were still heralding the morning. We returned to Barranco at night.

T H I S O N E was an Englishman who fished with a reed. On his long terra-cotta face, a high, thick nose; below, the mouth of a priest, drawn and immobilized, the sunken lips; and a Catacaos cigar; and one shaved hand; and a long, long, long reed ... Undoubtedly, this Englishman was like all fishermen, an idiot, yet his legs did not sway; instead, he stood upon the support rail, as slippery as a moss-covered tile. What did this Englishman fish, a furtive flash of light or minuscule *tramboyos?* I think he spent hour after hour fishing for a piece of seaweed with a drop of water on its tail that would swell, then collapse before he could catch it. A poet? Nothing of the sort: a travel agent from Dawson and Brothers LTD; but he fished with a reed. And the temptation to push him, and the Catacaos floating, and the reed cloven into the sandy bottom like a topmast.

I

  N T H E bewitched mirror of the rainy street – a drop of milk, the street lamp's iridescent globe; a drop of water, the sky above; a drop of blood, one's self for this foolish joy at unannounced winter's arrival . . . I am now that man with no age or race who appears in geography monographs, with ridiculous clothes, a somber countenance, his arms spread open as he directs Indian ink pastures and charcoal clouds – the engraving's sparse, ragged landscape – here is the West; North is toward that wall; South is behind me. That way to Asia. This way to Africa. Everything beyond the mountains or the sea suddenly approaches, meridian by meridian, in a man, through the brown waters of the causeway. The Turk is the Levant and the Occident, a tightly bound sheaf of latitudes: the face is Spanish; the pants, French; the nose, Roman; the eyes, German; the tie, Belgian; the bales of hay, Russian; the restlessness, Jewish. . . . As we travel to the East, the numbers increase. To the West, they decrease. Dakar or Peking. A haremesque joy as the blue cloth appears through the lattice with its drab edges of black rubber. The fields, with their rash of ancient burial grounds, at the road's open mouth. Fading light of falling drizzle. Trees with wet birds. There is a reason the earth is round. . . . And these cars, soiled by haste, by pride, by mud . . . The fig trees make the houses grow in their illusion of muddy and mossy foliage, almost water, almost water, water above, and below, sediments, chlorophyllous and clay, whatever. . . . Swallows, grasshoppers. One might even open one's round, ichthyological eyes. In the water, under water, the lines break up, the reflections are at the mercy of the surface. No, at the mercy of the force that moves it. But it's the same thing, after all. Asphalt pavement, a fine and fragile mica lamina . . . A very narrow street that widens, contracting from beginning to end like a pharynx so that two vehicles – one cart and a second cart – can continue together one beside the other. Everything is thus: tremulous, dark, as if on a movie screen.

To RAMON, a minuscule, barren jacaranda tree never looked like an Englishwoman with glasses. In vain a somewhat crazy photophobic gringa photographer – the pride of a rooming house with cretonne drapes and clean liners – wandered around Barranco day and night. The gringa was a moving road, sun-blind, leading to the tundra, to a nation of snow and moss where a gaunt, gray city of skyscrapers looms as mysterious as machinery in a dark factory. Miss Annie Doll's life needed to be loaded onto a sleigh and an airplane, an automobile and a trans-atlantic liner. And at the end of it, Miss Annie Doll was a reddish wax candle suckled on a sterilized bottle. Synthetic milk, canned meat, hard liquor, seven years in a sports academy, reindeer and squirrels, trips to China, archaeological collections in a suitcase from Manchester that holds all of civilization, aspirin tablets, the smell of sawdust in hotel dining rooms, the smell of smoke on the high seas, on board. . . . You evoke so many things, photo-phobic gringa photographer, you who lives in a rooming house, an enormous building with its third floor of gray planks, with its sadness of a railroad station and a chicken coop! Gringa, shel-tered road leading to the tundra, to Vladivostok, to Montreal, to the South Pole, to the perpetual winter of whitewashed scienti-fic academies, to anywhere at all . . .

But Ramon does not see your image enhanced by the sun in the jacaranda. To him, you are a somewhat crazy gringa, and a jacaranda is a tree that produces many purple flowers. You are a red, long, sinewy, mobile thing that carries a Kodak over its shoulder and asks questions that are wise, useless, and nonsensi-cal. . . . A jacaranda is a solemn, old-fashioned, confidential, ex-pressive, gaudy, mindful, family tree. You: almost a woman; a jacaranda: almost a man. You: human, in spite of everything; it: a tree, when we leave off the poetry.

Ramon, I'm not thinking about those splendid jacarandas in the park. Miss Annie Doll's only relationship to them is as their antithesis: a vegetable antithesis full of nature and supreme truth. But there stands a jacaranda on a secluded street that smells of bananas: a zigzagging street full of laundries; an alley-way lined with whitewashed walls without windows or doors that have the aura of a military hospital or a recently inaugurated school building. And the jacaranda on that street is the one I say is the gringa, or I don't know if it is a jacaranda that is the gringa or if it is the gringa that is a jacaranda. Whether the tree is very young or very old I don't know. Facing it we have the same doubts as when we face the pieces of pottery in the museums, not knowing if they are from Nasca or Chimu, authentic or falsified, black or white. Perhaps the jacaranda on Mott Street is both young and old at the same time, like the gringa – lanky, almost completely naked, with just one foliated arm, with one stump of purple flowers, free, as if blown there by the wind. Ramon, remember. We have gone, many an afternoon, to Mott Street to hear the church bells of Angelus Vespertine: iridescent soap bubbles that the puerile Saint Francis shoots through blowguns from the church towers into a child's sky. Ramon, don't you remember how the bells would burst above us? How from them came neither sight nor sound, just the cold smell of water, much too brief and bright for us to notice at the moment it wet our faces that were turned towards the darkening sky? The sunset was an overripe banana behind the Elysian bananas of Mott Street. But let's forget about the jacaranda and the church bells of Saint Francis. Let's remember Miss Annie Doll, tourist and photographer, a spring dressed in a jersey that sprang out of this Peruvian resort town's box of surprises. You pushed a button, and Miss Annie Doll's body and yellow glasses popped out. The toy was a local attraction, not for sale, belonging to everyone, absolutely public. The city and Miss Annie Doll . . . She lived on an income that came from far away, from fabulously far away, like a box of tea; she spoke a Latin that broke her clean porcelain teeth into a thousand smithereens like crystals; she failed to understand the bells of Saint Francis because she opted to hear them in Hebrew, and Saint Francis did not know dead languages, only how to blow soap bubbles to cheer up God; she wore glasses with the same tortoiseshell frames as yours, only the lenses in hers were yellow, antiluminous. And you, Ramon, are not a high-strung boy, nor do you suffer from conjunctivitis. Ramon, a normal boy . . . But the gringa, whether you like it or not, essentially . . . I guess . . . looks like the jacaranda on Mott Street.

On THE streetcar. Seven-thirty in the morning. A glimpse of the sun below the lowered shades. Tobacco smoke. An upright old lady. Two unshaven priests. Two clerks. Four typists, their laps full of notebooks. One schoolboy: I. Another schoolboy: Ramon. The smell of beds and creosote. The color of the sun reposes on the windowpane from outside like a cloud of pale, translucent butterflies. A sudden excess of passengers. A sinister old lady with skin like crepe, like the crepe of her shawl, where Ramon was sitting. Ramon, hanging from a door – the driver's door – turns his head and his eyes in opposite directions. Ramon's glasses reflect a meek philosophical splendor. Ramon carries the last afternoon – yesterday afternoon – in his satchel. He is going to school, because he is late, and he is late, because he is going to school. I go with him, near him, secretly chagrined that my feet may not reach the ground. Yet, on the contrary, I can hold in my oversized hand the spines of all my textbooks. And this is a pleasure, almost a consolation, at my pedantic fourteen years of age. My life hangs from the score on my first test as a crumb of bread hangs from a spider's web. Ramon suddenly reaches over a bald head to hand me an engraving that shows an angel with a constipated look on its face and a twilight that is, first and foremost, roguish. A gift from Catita: eenie, meenie, miney, mo, boarding school nonsense, pranks of nuns, and a long jump rope that creates afternoon ellipses. Catita, date of a desert palm tree . . . But the gentleman only enjoys dates from the palm trees pruned by "*Mamere*": the only dates the unlikely Mr. Chaplain graciously accepts come in a small basket with a perfect white silk bow on the handle: lying butterflying. Innocent dates, Palestinian dates . . . The outskirts of Lima. An oil factory swells its greasy belly and belches like a drunk old lady: Lima. The police toss back and forth from uniform to uniform an infant whistle that screeches and covers its eyes with its fists. Suddenly, the shadow of the school building gets in my eyes like the night.

MY FIRST love was twelve years old and had black fingernails. In that little town with eleven thousand inhabitants and a publicity agent for a priest, my then-Russian soul rescued the ugliest girl from her solitude with a grave, social, somber love that was like the closing session of an international worker's congress. My love was vast, dark, sluggish, had a beard, glasses, and portfolios, with sudden incidents, twelve languages, police ambushes, problems all over the place. She would say to me, when things became sexual, "You are a socialist." And her little soul – that of a pupil of European nuns – opened like a personal prayer book to the page about mortal sin.

My first love left me, repelled by my socialism and my foolishness. "I hope you all don't end up being socialists. . . . " And she swore she'd give herself to the first true Christian who came her way, even if he wasn't yet twelve years old. Once I was alone, I gave up on my transcendent problems and fell truly in love with my first love. I felt a toxicomaniacal, agonizing need to inhale, until my lungs burst, her smell: the smell of a small school, of India ink, of enclosed spaces, of sun in the patio, of government-issued paper, of aniline, of coarse cotton cloth worn against the skin – the smell of India ink, skinny and black – almost an ebony ruling pen, a ghost of the holidays. And that was my first love.

My second love was fifteen years old. A crybaby with missing teeth, braids of hemp, freckles all over her body, without family, without ideas, with too much future, with excessive femininity. My rival was a celluloid and rag doll that did nothing but laugh at me with its stupid, rascally jowls. I had to understand an endless amount of perfectly unintelligible things. I had to say an endless amount of perfectly unsayable things. I had to get one hundreds on my exams – a suspect, shameful, ridiculous score; the chicken before the egg. I had to see her, imitate her dolls. I had to hear her cry for me. I had to suck on candies of different colors and flavors. . . . My second love abandoned me like in a tango. An evil man . . .

My third love had beautiful eyes and very coquettish, almost *cocotte* legs. Required reading was Friar Luis de Leon and Carolina Invernizzio. Wayward girl . . . I can't imagine why she fell in love with me. I consoled myself for her irrevocable decision to be my friend after almost being my lover with the twelve spelling errors in her last letter.

My fourth love was Catita.

My fifth love was a dirty girl with whom I sinned almost at night, almost in the sea. The memory of her smells almost as she smelled, of shadows in a movie theater, of a wet dog, of underwear, of baked goods, of hot bread, superimposed odors, and, each one on its own, almost disagreeable, like frosting on cakes, ginger, meringue, et cetera. The collection of smells made of her a true temptation for a seminary student. Dirty, dirty, dirty . . . My first mortal sin . . .

T HE PORT, with its necklace of lights and its husky silhouette of love for the serious and not at all spendthrift man, remained behind. Fifty thousand souls, and a very distant, very distant joy on the other side of the port – the sea's enormous curve, the Panama Canal, the Atlantic Ocean, Grace Liners, and the etceteras of destiny. Suddenly – he knew not how – Paris. And sixty chapters of a novel he had been writing on board: one thousand pages blackened by letters that threatened Miguel's sanity, mad things, shouting, all without any motive. His sports coat stiffened and tensed at that bundle of conflict and hysteria. Because the novel was a conflict of hysterias – a woman threw herself in the arms of a millionaire, and he bit her chin. Astral autobiography, I suppose ... A silent bus made of springs and elastic bands carried Miguel through a flood of speed and darkness to the hotel. A gust of fog, cold, drizzle, and benzine blew out the curtain and left upon the windowsill the whiff of a phonograph – rubbers, adultery, home remedies. . . . A stork would have left a child in an unmarried woman's bed in this way: the result of a mistake, fatigue, a joke. . . . Like in Barranco, no more and no less. He got undressed. Once naked, he did not know what to do; he wanted to go out, return to Lima, do nothing. He got into bed – early, bored, indolent – and fell fast asleep. In a moment he was back in Lima, on the Jiron de la Union, at twelve noon. Ramon was carried through side streets in a mud-splattered Hudson with frighteningly shaky, half-crazed windows. A mobile fig tree strolled down a street crowded with seminarians, streetwalkers, and geometry professors – a thousand aging gentlemen, dirty collars, a long hand. Manuel awoke, and now it was Paris with its smell of asphalt and its factory sounds and its public pleasures. Manuel visited Latin American consulates; in the Louvre, under the grotesqueries of colors, a sentimental *cocotte* left one of her rough and dry hands between both of his, cadaverous; in the Moulin Rouge he sinned twice; on the Bridge of Alexander III, a star from Lima smiled at him from the edge of the brim of his hat. And one day – he did not know how – he awoke in Lima, wrapped in his sky blue blanket, his wings limpid under his guardian angel. Now it was Lima with its smell of sun and guano and its private pleasures. Manuel did not know what to do; return to Paris, go out, do nothing. . . . So he fell back into a deep sleep.

T HE SLOPE of the cliff plunged into fig trees, moist earth, trenches, moss, vines, Japanese pavilions, from top to bottom, from the parish church to the beach. Suddenly, the sinister, rampant road twisted. And on a covered sled – on one side, light; on the other, a make-believe cavern and an invisible madonna and a miracle of candles that burn under dripping gutters – it fell onto the platform. An old-time tenderness played on the piano things of Duncher Lavalle, and a violin hid its voice behind an obese, unknown, Italian millionaire. An old man, down below, in the sea, sprinkled those interested in his bald spot with the water that flowed from his hands out of his round, hollow arms; and the old man was a suction pump and two parish priestly hands, forgiving and jovial. Here one might want to hang signs on the indifferent doors covered with Venetian blinds: "No sinning in the hallways." "Bathers are asked to refrain from speaking English." "Total destruction of the place is not permitted." "Et cetera." Here one is possessed by a certain kind of frenetic and infantile, experienced and weary, critical and dilettantish culture. Paul Morand on a sailing boat accompanied by his earless, raceless lover on their way to Siam. Like in the social pages. Cendrars, who comes to Peru to preach the enthusiasms of a spontaneous Bavarian explorer (lynched tourists, wheat plantations, and the man who strangles his destiny). Radiquet, carrying around on tiptoe his wife who is suddenly uglified by a heroic husband. Istrati, a whiff of Dutch cheese, a ships's hold, Eurasian misery. All the same, all indistinct, unaffiliable – secretaries of embassies, heirs to textile mills, day students in schools run by European nuns, failed university students, devout women who have come for their health, for a saintly scandal, a spiritual experience. Excessive Baedeker, a guide from who knows which avant-garde Pentapolis, inadmissible nationalism, a great big hunch ... A drunken Charleston shakes up a buxom lady as if she were a sack full of wood chips. A policeman rubs his anointed, cunning hands. The funicular modernly lends its signature to the cliff's prerepublican calling. Lima, Lima, finally ... And everything is nothing but your insanity and a Peruvian resort for bathing in the sea. And a native and premature desire that Europe will make of us men, women's men, terrible Portuguese men, men like Adolphe Menjou, with a false moustache and a valet, with an international smile and a dozen London gestures, with specific danger and a thousand unexpected vices, with two Rolls Royces and a German liver ailment. Nothing else. Bad Nauheim, Cauterets, summer in Paris ... Nothing of the kind.

SHE WORE a parochial blouse and had a very polite index finger. Public school teacher. Twenty-eight years old. Perfect health. Christian resignation to spinsterhood. Her face was very white. Her nose was very fragile. And a little pair of glasses attached to her right ear with a delicate gold chain. And above all, Reuter Soap – a white, pedagogical smell. The skin on her nose was finer and more sensitive than that on any other part of her body, though no one could actually prove this. But, oh phoo ... the world also knew that she would never get married and no one could prove this before the fact and, nevertheless, it was true. The truth! ... the enthusiasm of a missionary priest, the

theme of a frantic cuckold, the worst part of a good book, anything, except the skin of a twenty-eight-year old pedagogue.
True? Her nose filled her glasses with difficulties: they were a lap
dog that barked reflections. Modern manners and the news in
La Prensa also made her nose wrinkle, but less, less. . . . At seven
in the morning her face blossomed – unexpected, unexpectable
flower – a begonia plant in a green pot at her window, on her
window sill, in her house, in her house, in her house. "Pin, pin,
Saint Augustine" . . . Then her face ended just above the long,
sturdy, firm body of a guardian angel, a prudent virgin, a volun-
tary miss. With an awkward rustle of sheets in her chamber – the
silly, useless fluttering of a caged goose – the daily life of
Señorita Muler began, a negation of the treasury, a woman of
her house, domestic, long, soft, intimate, and cold like a pillow
at six o'clock postmeridian. Señorita Muler did everything well:
with silence, indifference, reluctance. At breakfast she held her
cup between her thumb and index finger, like on a date, and her
whole hand turned into an essential, hard, intelligent claw. And
her index finger, more crooked than ever, acquired virtue, exoti-
cism, smiles, the sadness of a former Russian duke waiting tables
in Berlin. At nine in the morning, at the stroke of the clock's bell
Señorita Muler instantly became a public school teacher; basic
education, the pillars of the state; she said no and made her
hands into a little ball. In the afternoon, Señorita Muler submit-
ted herself to the sounds, the sights, and the smells, and spun poetry with the wingtips of her legs and arms, ivory forever brand
new like an elephant's gums. Possible nonsense from a preco-
cious old maid: ubiquity, crown and scepter, a heavenly
meadow, to be a bird with the head of a carnation, to die a saint,
to go to Paris . . . Asleep, she dreamt of Napoleon riding a
green horse and of Santa Rosa de Lima. She cried only when she
had a handkerchief. She would say, "Bon Dieu," and laugh, up

and down the scale, lackadaisically. She did not understand Eguren, but she recognized him when she saw him. She would mumble, "Out of the question" . . . her eyes far away. And: "With much pleasure." And, "Jesus, Jesus . . . " She would place half of her finger perpendicular over the page of the book she was reading. Et cetera. Señorita Muler dreamt about him one night, three days after having met him. His shift came before Ramon's; a colonel who won the War of the Pacific – a patriotic dream from a nationalistic textbook. Ramon finally penetrated Señorita Muler's subconscious; and one night my favorite friend became a priest; he hailed from Palestine on Mister Kakison's back. Lima turned into a tangled heap of towers; the ringing of bells fell like stones in a labyrinth of dirt clods; an Italian angel sang in Latin; a Boy Scout trumpet called only to men of good will; the Jordan River escaped while laughing at the sky through the squinted eye of Viceroy Superunda's congenial bridge; Ramon, wearing the habit of the Order of Mercy and with the moon of Barranco in his hands, appeased the elements and coughed horribly. Señorita Muler fell in love with Ramon. Ramon did not fall in love with Señorita Muler. Señorita Muler was twenty-eight years old; Ramon, eighteen, but, in spite of it all, Ramon did not fall in love with Señorita Muler. From a million points of view, in a long tango like a movie reel, the phonograph recorded the resort town in slow motion – yellowed and desolate like a Mexican village in a cowboyesque soap opera of Tom Mix. And, behind it all, the sea, useless and absurd like a bandstand the morning after the afternoon of a sports event. And a triangle of vulgar pigeons carried off Señorita Muler's pen strokes in their beaks, romantically.

A GERMAN wearing thick-soled shoes and smelling of leather and disinfectant rented a room full of spider webs in Ramon's house. There was another one, freshly wallpapered and also to let, but the one with spider webs had a large window facing the neighbor's garden, with a view of elderberry trees and a plaster of Paris Eros with a terrible parrot perched on its head. A swallow that was hunting fleas between the floorboards when Herr Oswald Teller, with rapt attention, looked over the room for the first time with the round magnifying glass on his forehead, convinced him to rent it without delay, fearing that some Herr Hemmer or another Herr Dabermann would find out that a room with swallows and a garden with a plaster Love and sea breezes was for rent. The morning after the afternoon, Ramon's sleep-filled and unbespectacled eyes saw the portrait of Bismarck, the violin, the gaiters, the rucksack, the seven languages, the microscope, the crucifix, the mug for Herr Oswald Teller's beer, all descend from the cart, for he was changing his place of residence *mit Kind und Kegel,* with everything he owned. Finally Herr Oswald Teller himself, fat and wet like the morning, descended from the cart in person. He walked along beside it, his tiny legs getting tangled in the tail bristles of the mule that pulled the flatbed cart. Martinita: an enormous, old mule, fussy like an in-law . . . And Herr Oswald Teller spoke to the carter about the mornings in Hanover, the full moon, the industrialization of America, the Battle of the Marne. . . . and his *rr*s rose from his belly, and his glances flowed from his brain, and his memories skated around on the bluish snow. And Herr Oswald Teller left off talking when Martinita left off pulling. Joaquin, as sullen and hermetic as a Javanese idol, chewed on his black cud and imagined the sea, remote and perpendicular, in the sea of fog between his mule's ears. The fog of the sea smelled of shellfish, and the sea hung in the fog. Over the sidewalk fell a dark, dense, delicate, brief rain of German illustrated magazines, *Fliegende Blatter, Garten,* and *Laube,* magazines with covers displaying horrible, cosmic nudes, fierce euphoria over architectural painting, Wagnerianizing. . . . Then everything was in Herr Oswald Teller's room. Herr Oswald Teller found a place for everything. The cry of the milkmaid fell unexpectedly into the middle of the room, and a few minutes later, so did the church bells ringing six times at six o'clock in the morning. Herr Oswald Teller stuffed the six bells of six in the morning into the pocket of his hunting jacket, and the cry of the milkmaid grabbed him by the brush with which he brushed his bald spot.

(One day, Herr Oswald Teller told Ramon that, when he brushed his hair, he felt happy, smelled the stables, and imagined himself in Hanover; and the milkmaid's cry was still a reflection of blue, peaceful, peasant light on the brush.) In the afternoons, in the long pre-nights to Lima's winter, Herr Oswald Teller, from his mildewy room, flooded the house with music and homesickness and geniality. Liquified Mozart descended the staircase and formed puddles in the hollows like a torrent of rain that had soaked through the roof. Ramon fumed. Classical concert ... Brrr ... Old music, intransigent, imposed on the admiration of a twenty-year-old, by dint of a warning, horrible grandmotherly warnings full of good sense ... And Ramon drifted away in his armchair and hardened, and listened, and in the end grew dizzy with a magic flute in his eardrums.

L ULU wore a robe like a cabbage leaf, cool and stiff. The spinster-doll colors on her face were too bright. She obviously needed to be allowed to age, to fade. One had the urge to hang her out in the sun by her braid. Lulu was the terror of the parochial lay-sisters — she sowed the benches of the temple with thumbtacks, poured holy water on the faithful, made the sexton fall in love with her, disturbed the chorus, tripped over everyone's feet, and extinguished all the candles ... And she was good: a pure little soul who sought only to make God happy with her mischief. Lulu was a saint in her own way. And in the midst of the stubborn and stuffy saints in the ecclesiastical mode, Lulu's wild and human saintliness stood out like a blackberry bramble over a cauliflower patch.

T HE PROMENADE atop the sea cliff of Barranco, the last stretch on the way to Chorrillos, zigzagging, seascape in relief, chiseled with a knife, a sailor's toy, so different from the promenade of Chorrillos, too much light, an excessive horizon, obese sky under the sea's care. The promenade of Chorrillos, superpanorama with a fourth dimension, solitude ... And the whole sea changes with the promenade – this one, a transatlantic cruise ship; that one, route to Asia; the other, first love. And the sea is Salgari's river or one of Loti's shores, or Verne's fantastic ship, and the sea is never pale green, but has zones that are gray, colorless, lined with the tracks of ducks; full of minute coasts and feeble backgrounds. The sea is a soul we once had, that we cannot find, that we barely remember as our own, a soul that is different along each promenade. And the sea is never the cold and vigorous one that squeezed us, in estival lust, during our childhood and our vacations. The promenade is full of wolf-dogs and English nursemaids, a domestic sea, family histories, the great-grandfather was captain of a frigate, or a freebooter in the sea of the Antilles, a bearded millionaire. A promenade with ancient gardens of fragile roses and dirty and dwarfed palm trees; a fox terrier barks at the sun; the solitude of the huts appears at the windows to contemplate noontime; an unemployed worker, and the light, the light of the sea, humid and warm. Promenade with patches of dry grass; the tension before our first date with a girl we don't really love; above this promenade is a diverse sky that collides with the one over the sea. Promenade with one hour of quietude: six o'clock in the afternoon; the two twin skies, one without a solution that has continuity, both with the same gulls and melancholies.

AMPLE, hard, firm end-of-February sun. There is no shadow possible in this immutable, exact, artificial midday. Night will never arrive. It is two o'clock in the afternoon, and the sun is still halfway across the sky, stuck in a stubborn and foolish affinity with the earth. The plaster along the streets gleams – the white, the yellow, the light green, the sky blue, the pearly gray – the perfect, prudent colors of the houses of Barranco. There is only the scent of heat, only heat – a solid scent of fully dilated air. Brass and tiles clang in the windows. Flagless poles with a dangling rope that forms a knot on top of the cornice. The one o'clock bells dissolve their borax of sound into the spongy air, and over Barranco descends a flutter of school-children, light whiteness, the moment's feathers that fly off to sea. The end of the lunch hour, the streets' solitude, and a silvery hot and cold silence, and the shimmering of causeways paved with round, auriferous stones, with stones from riverbeds, thirsty and gasping. A cart carries off, in its squeaking and banging the fever of the streets through which it has traveled: nightmares, beings, banana groves, bitterness, deaf systolic and diastolic contractions. . . . The sultry air isochronously strikes the eardrums of the window glass – tense, pained membranes. And in the wake of the cart, the avenue remains pale, convalescent, without ailments and without health. And the cart continues past the walls to burn up the evil of the streets in the blaze of the distant sunset. A memory of banana groves . . . Each sound collides with the hard air, and there is a bang. Three in the afternoon. And a trolley car sings its heart out with the guitar of the road to Miraflores, gray, convivial, sad, two metal strings, and around its neck, the green belt of the *alameda* that beats the sea air. Streetcar, sambo casanova . . .

S H E   S H O U T E D at me that she loved me with her entire face, fresh and covered more than ever with lint from her towel; naked, cold, and juicy in yellow overalls like the inside of oranges; she almost fell into my arms – an adverse wind prevented it; I told her she was as terrifying and inoffensive as a sea lion; she did not believe me; her gluteal, livid knees trembled; I reproached her for her impertinence, her immodesty, her bad faith, her bare feet that could get hurt; she warned me that she bit like *tramboyos* when caught, and she showed me her fishbowl teeth; she could also scratch, like hunted otters – she slowly unsheathed her nails – not at all cornaceous: rather misty, opaque;

she allowed me not to get frightened; we went down to the beach, I think on a rope, like cats on coasting steamboats; we returned to the gazebo in the water; she measured the craziness in my eyes with her own; with a frown she tightened the straps of her nakedness over her pale shoulders; she was trying to say to me, as if to a naughty child: "Settle down, or you won't get a snack . . . ," but she was afraid of making me cry. My thorax – that of a studious boy – dissuaded her words; she forgave me; she became natural; the cold x-rayed her thighs and bound her arms together; she looked out beyond the circular pier; suddenly, in a stupendous, incomprehensible parable, she threw herself into the bather's semisea, head first behind her inverted wig that hung like the tentacles of an octopus on a grappling iron in the market. I had to wait for her on the beach, under the terrace – semidarkness of marine cavern – amidst wholesalers – hairy, vertical, shivering cetaceans – and the stench of seafood – green humors; she came out of her drenching dressed in water; she no longer loved me; the two of us, under the platform; I thought of a caustic and pretty jellyfish, but no . . . I grabbed her hand that was as slippery as a fish; I dragged her along toward the light and the desert in a painful race over round pebbles; my heels grew numb; our entwined hands ran into a useless, upright rail that balanced a foolish rock on its end, and we separated; she wanted to be a rail that could not be dragged along the beach just like that; a mercurial lizard carried away one of her sad glances; she wanted to forgive me with all her heart and I would not allow it; the garment of moisture fell off her; she hit the beach with her knees and said no. . . .

T HIS AFTERNOON, the world is a potato in a sack. The sack is a small, white, dusty sky, like the small sacks used for carrying flour. The world is little, dark, gritty, as if just harvested in some unknown agricultural infinity. I have gone to the countryside to see the clouds and the alfalfa fields. But I have gone almost at night, and I will no longer be able to smell the smells of the afternoon, tactile, that are smelled through the skin. Out of its dusty whiteness, the sky – affiliated with the vanguard – creates round, multicolored clouds that at times look like German balls and at others, really, like the clouds of Norah Borges. Now I have to smell colors. And the road I take turns into a crossroads. And the four pathways born to the road screech like new-born babes: they want to be rocked; and the wind turns into a swinging young dandy after nightfall and does not want to rock roads: the air puts on oxford trousers, and there is no way to convince it that it is not a man. I walk away from sky. And, as I leave the countryside, surrounded by urbanizations, I notice that the countryside is in the sky: a flock of fat, fleecy clouds – award winners at the Exposition – romp about in the green sky. And this I see from far away, so far away that I get into bed to sweat colors.

A FTERNOONS were white in winter, and in summer, a reddish gold, gold increasing into sun, a sun that filled the entire sky. Winter afternoons were white, the luminous and piercing whiteness of salt crystals, and the sun therein was a silvery sun with a dented circumference. But in March there was a Monday with a pink afternoon, an afternoon of decadence in the style of D'Annunzzio, and everybody was deeply moved by the pink afternoon. Long lines of thin-blooded old ladies – black scarves wrapped around yellow necks with red tendons (potbellied old men accompanied by their nameless friends), the current price of cotton, hairy hands wearing wedding rings, and lenses, and glasses, and spectacles, and spherical eyelids, and wrinkles that looked painted on. Suddenly, the pinkness turned red; and the sunset became a common sunset; and the audience at the celestial movie house voiced their disapproval at the change of program. Weren't they showing *Divino amor*? The story was by D'Annunzzio, the hero was Fiume's; some bald dago who wrote verses; an unlikely man; an Italian national fantasy; an aviator; a wreck; an author appearing in the Index; a show that must not be missed . . . Valentino . . . Dream landscapes . . . Passion, sacrifice, jealousy, a sumptuous wardrobe, high society . . . And suddenly, nothing! The vulgar epic poem of the summer, the red sky, the sun sky, and the night as a shout. The respectable audience fiercely stamped its feet as it withdrew in an orderly fashion befitting people who know their rights, serious people, honorable people. Suddenly the sky donned the come-look-and-see attitude of a shopkeeper, and then there was no sun no summer no anything: just a buttocks in the air, an enormous buttocks reddened by a lengthy sitting. The audience swore it would appeal to the mayor. On Matti Street, the fig trees went quickly to sleep so they could get up early. At a window, a very old piano was dying of love, like the Duke of Hohemburg – pink bald spot, white sideburns – in one or another of Kallmann's operettas.

W E SWAM in the sea and the afternoon, to the
left of the setting sun that was concealed by the pier as if it were
something the city had forbidden and that could lead to the
resort's closure. Lala's mother clung to a strong wave at high
tide, a violent wave, maned and clumsy like a buffalo – the poor
woman looked through the foam for one of her hands that had
been carried off by the wave. The previous day – a cold, malignant yesterday – one of her tennis shoes had gotten lost; by the
time she noticed her bare foot – when she stepped on an under-
water gringo – the shoe was no longer afloat, for it was a rubber
shoe; the gringo's head – a diver's shapeless head – surfaced;

Lala's mother said she was sorry; the gringo did not understand; her mother nodded *yes,* to herself, quickly, between two large waves. Her mother had found her lost hand between those of a nearby Arab who was glad that even though he was an Arab he was allowed to swim, et cetera. Lala showed me the nipple of one of her breasts. I hid in the sea. Lala could already have been my girlfriend. Her mother rose like a submarine. In a bathing suit, she simply was not herself. The legs of the bottoms and the sleeves of the top were bloated with water. With the purple tip of her tongue, she subdued a red lock of wet hair that traversed her face from her hairline to her chin like a scar. Her shoulder was tightly bound with a scapular as if for a bloodletting. The old woman defied the bathhouse, waged war on the sea, and cast a shadow over the shadow under the platform. The ocean sea descended. Above, in a section of the sky that was blue, the waxing moon blinked with the frustrated high tide. The stones that had escaped with a horrible din from the path taken by Lala's mother came to rest at our feet, excited, friendly. The sand rushed underfoot — it wanted to knock us down and carry us out to the high seas as if we were seashells. Lala stuck her forefingers in her ears; her eyes and teeth chattered. Suddenly, unprovoked, I kissed her behind a large, sickly, complacent wave that did not advance; the kiss resounded through the afternoon like in a theater. There were black and green patches on the water. The railings of the pier broke and disintegrated below into fillets of shadows, shadows of fish, patches of shadow. . . . Everything seemed on the verge of collapse: the sky with its horizon in flames; the sea full of tidal gaps; the pier with its girders that dissolved into the sea. I did not love Lala. My fingers were wrinkled, stiff. Lala blew on them the warm, humid breath of a hairdresser's spray. We emerged from our swim as from bed, as from a dream. . . . Lala yawned.

I IMAGINE that man as a vague presence from which hung a badly cut coat. A few words in Ramon's diary attempt, in vain, to reconstruct in my mind the destroyed, dissipated image of the man. "Dog eyes in a face of wax, so full of a sweetness that was nothing but indifference. And one of his index fingers – on the right hand, the stiff finger of idlers, of canons, of boys – yellowed by tobacco. And the ashen moustache with golden handlebars that seemed to burst from his nasal passages like a heavy cloud of pitch . . . And the trousers, empty holes, with large bulges at the knees . . . " So states Ramon's diary, the notebook with a black oilskin cover filled with words that I don't know how ended up in the hands of Señorita Muler, Preceptor and Directress of the Republic of Haiti Educational Center. Ah! Muler's hands . . . ! How they moved about among the classroom gossip and the cardboard grammar books – the rudiments of geography with angelic purity, fantastic self-confidence! But those notes, I don't know if they truly reflected Ramon's image of that man or were simply nonsense that descended into my friend's fingers while he wrote in his diary, and there turned into the foolish desire to make a point. Did that man ever exist? Is it possible that Ramon and I simply dreamed him up? Created him out of someone else's features and his own gestures? Did that man have memory, understanding, and will? . . . Because I can now see the details Ramon mentions arranging themselves in a human form in the atmosphere of a dense and yellow summer. I also see that man dispersed, incomplete, part-crazy, part-environment, part-real, with his belly of air, and his calves of the marine horizon, vertical, charading, vexed, bordering the edge of the promenade without a railing. Perhaps everything is nothing but the essential elements, physiognomic dates, crosses and capital letters, the shorthand of a wayfaring observer who at a particular moment re-created in Ramon's fat and long-haired head the image of that man who did, in fact, exist. I now feel the desire to have that man in front of me in order to ask him some weighty questions whose answers would reveal the humanity or inhumanity of the subject: "Do you support Leguia? What brand of cigarettes do you smoke? Do you keep a mistress? Do you suffer from the heat?" If that man answered that he was a monarchist, that he did not smoke because he did not have a narghile, that he loved a pious old woman, that he only suffered from the heat in winter, then I could know for a certainty that we, Ramon and I, had created that man during an hour of idleness and twilight, while the sun rolled silently and quickly through a concave sky, red and green like a Milanese ball. There is no doubt that there are men who are nothing more than their empty trousers. There are children who are nothing but the joy of a sailor's hat: children who are not even the hat they wear. There are women who are barely a false hand in an ass-hide purse. Priests who are barely the wrinkle of their cassock. What is that man?

P

OST-MIDDAY, vapors of the sun and romping about out of puerile boredom . . . Catita, evil heart . . . There is nothing to do, nothing to think about, nothing to desire. Catita, evil heart . . . But now, Catita, nothing matters to me. A street illuminated by silence – down it go these eyes of ours, our eyes, heedless and curious children. And we are struck blind. And a waft of a *yaravi* ballad with its air of the highlands brings a chill to the street. Afterwards, nothing, not even ourselves – you and I, Fernando, devout face and long pants.

Night, hairy and taciturn dogs . . . The dirty desire to climb trees that, as a joke, have bloomed with a star – a mocking, bantering, bursting star; fig tree, fig, in its autumn of shade. Afraid of the bogeyman with the face of a mother-in-law. Catita, cold bed . . . Streets under electric lights, a cart's nightmare, squat houses with fabulous palm trees . . . And a shattered silence that is a mortal sin.

Clean and decent morning with recently washed foliage. Sometimes a rural breeze that seems to come, oddly enough, from the windows, passes by carrying the sweet smell of vegetables. But this is a breeze that escapes at the first corner. And the air returns to its clear, clean, empty state. A pretty Indian woman, with her hard, shiny, damp head of hair – a mud carving – walks along absorbed in her own thoughts, watching her breasts bounce, tremble, bounce . . . A cook. Her calves – firm, ugly – turn her white cotton socks gray. She left her baby in the kitchen. And there is no doubt that now she is not thinking about him: now she is only thinking about herself, about her breasts she is watching tremble, bounce. Rarified air. The trolley cars pass in vain: nothing is heard.

W E READ the Spaniards, and nobody but the Spaniards. Only Raul looked through French, English, and Italian books in translations by someone named Perez, or Gonzalez de Mesa, or Zapata or Zapater. This is how, in spite of Belda and Azorin, we had a picturesque image of universal literature. This is how we learned about the life – eternal like Our Father's – of that poor Stephan Dedalus: "an interesting man who wore glasses and wet his bed." In this way we found out about the trick played on a good theater director by six characters, how they enticed him to write and then ended up not existing. This is how we found out about a young man who tried to be a disciple of the Devil, as if the Devil would demean himself by being a teacher. And strange names that were men – Shaw, Pirandello, Joyce – danced around on the tip of Raul's tongue: puppets bewitched by an illiterate witch. To know ourselves . . . Stephan Dedalus was not Joyce's Stephen Dedalus: Stephan Dedalus was, undoubtedly, an ambitious boy who dreamt of marrying a rich Yankee; a boy who was very intelligent and had a lot of self-confidence, so much so that he tricked a whole convent of Jesuits. As for Pirandello's son, he held the opinion that it had been immoral of the father – a cynical cuckold – to burden a son, about whom nothing bad was ever said, with a putative mother. Ramon bit his lip. The disciple of the Devil was a depraved and stubborn young man, and most likely beardless. We did not have a behaviorist concept of humanity. Joyce? An idiot. Pirandello . . . ? Another idiot. Shaw . . . ? A third idiot, even more of an idiot than the first two, what with his historical concept of literature, his bankrupt jokes, and his mania for always going against the grain; and especially, so chaste, so old, and so vegetarian; and especially, Irish, that is to say, English, in spite of the Pope and home rule.

All of us, except Raul, were steeped in the Spanish and American moldy literary stew. For, like on Sancho's Island of Barataria, it is the food of canons and rich men.

Let Wilde be the stuff of the curious who commit sins out of boredom. Let's welcome Don Jacinto Benavente's asexual confidants, with their pointed beards, parabolic bellies, and make-believe trousers; and also his priests that know how to behave in high society; his women who commit adultery under orders of their confessors; his perfectly humane and useless lives; his centripetal morals; his clichéd conversations, everything of Benavente's. And likewise with Fernan Caballero's literature, a credulous and fortunate literature with ecclesiastical license.

The same with Pardo Bazan's, literature that smells of an old lady's closet with vague whiffs of thyme, full of sins that are never committed – such pious intentions this author has! And Pereda's withered and uncouth literature, with his severe, somber, frowning girls that give themselves to their fellow men for the love of God. And Perez Galdos's practical and perilous literature with consumptives and the insane and criminals and the diseased, all of whom the reader sees from afar at no risk to himself. And Maeztu's: a table of logarithms that smells of aftershave in which everything fits as if it were a handbag from Manchester, everything condensed, of course, and full of ciphers, and as dignified as an English maid. And Camba's literature, a dialogue between a railroad and a young man without family, without work, without philosophies. And Father Coloma's, full of prudent and wary angels that don't let go of their zithers for a single moment, and of courtesans with good dispositions, and of advice for Catholic aristocrats. And Baroja's digestions, and Azorin's matinees, and Valle Inclan's eves, and Zamacois's nights. Everything, everything, just like that, as it comes, as it falls, but without inhumanities . . .

R AMON'S aunt swam for a long time. With one heavy hand she wet her tattered cap, and with the other, she subdued the waves. From time to time, a tennis shoe would emerge from her unsinkable bosom: it was a truant foot. She was an old woman who was afraid of the rocks: fat, humid, a good summer vacationer; she arrived at the first sign of heat and left at the last. She rented a rickety shack with a large window and an enormous window shade. A cat that looked like a Negress and a Negress that looked like a toy . . . The parish church behind and a phonograph made of tin and wood. The small patio was a basket full of yellowed papers. Ramon's aunt never read the newspapers. In her polka dot bathrobe, she could hear the toilet from the dining room. An old woman. Fat. She will return in December. Ramon, on the other hand, will never return.

Now the summer is really over. Summer and the pretext of summer – girls with happy legs, priests with dark circles under their eyes, the members of the Judicial Council, the heat, the holidays . . . The pretext . . . The pretexts . . . Now winter is upon us – an extracalendrical winter, orthodoxically Bergsonian: movies in twenty chapters. Lima, dirty Lima, equestrian, commercial, athletic, nationalistic, so serious . . . Now summer is really over. We have come, Lucho and I, to the midway promenade, the one we have baptized Proust Boulevard. Yes, Proust Boulevard – coastal, ancient, brave, outstanding – that is only a boulevard on one side – on the other, the psychological immensity of the sea – the side where stands the house of the Swann family, the door felt through each one of its molecules, the infinitesimal calculation of its emotional probabilities. Trees . . . ? – the street lamps – the trunks of shrubs the light twists and the shadows turn green. At six in the morning, at six in the evening, the street lamps are the most vegetable thing in the world, in an analytic, synthetic, scientific, passive, decisive, botanical, simple way – the upper edges of the trunks support crystal jars that hold yellow flowers. In the great hothouse of the dawn, in the household furnace of the dusk – dark rays, hypervegetation, observation, summary, skeleton, truth, exact temperature. But now it is not the sea along one side of a street from a French novel; the sea is now the sea of waves and little bits of daydreams for a spinster aunt. And, moreover, its colors – an extremely discreet sunset, the antithesis of a dawn that arrives on tiptoe, almost a pretty-girl morning, but without a kiss or a sign of the cross. Sunday and morning mass. The organ spreads through the fog like stones banging together in the water. Today there will be a plenilune, full moon, a starless night with a breach of light in the middle – a whole and glorious belly button. We shall not stop coming here at night. In the cup of coffee of the firmament will float, indissoluble, delicate, the lump of sugar of the moon. And all of it will be poetry, my friend. We shall prelive a superlife, perhaps actually future in which all men will be brothers and abstemious and vegetarians and theosophists and athletes. And that moon of sugar will turn into a horrible sweetness in our mouths. And a cloud the color of café au lait. What will it be? It might not be anything. Or perhaps it is a verse of Neruda. Or perhaps a symbolic coast, Amara's fatherland, Eguren's dream. Or, if you prefer, simply a cloud the color of café au lait – there's got to be a reason we are sixteen years old and have down on our upper lips. Tomorrow, a football match on the rough conch grass of who knows which field on the outskirts of Lima. Champion with tendinous and hairy mosaic legs, beak of the wingless, Byzantine angel in a cloud of dust, Romanian emigrant, stenographer-typist of the Dess Company, stock agents . . . And the whole match will be a stupid yet perfect plan of advance, in what appears to be the air, of a hard black ball picked up from the ground by an invisible rubber band. A pathetic, trivial, unlikely, cinematic summer of the newsreels. A Rolls runs off snorting along the paved road like a recently castrated world-renowned Swiss bull. And in that Rolls the summer left for the South Pole, carrying with it the already surpassed hope for that Argentinean October full of gulls – the last October we lived. To be happy for one day . . . We have already been happy for three whole months. And now, what should we do? Die? . . . Now you get sentimental. It is sane to become lyrical when life turns ugly. But it is still the afternoon – a matutinal, naive afternoon, with cold hands, with Western braids, serene and contented like a wife, but a wife who still has the eyes of a bride, but. . . . Come on, Lucho, tell tales of Quevedo, brutal copulations, hasty wedding, shocked nuns, chaste Englishwomen. . . . Say whatever comes to mind, let's play at psychoanalysis, follow old ladies, tell jokes. . . . Everything, anything but die.

Underwood Poems

HARD and magnificent prose of city streets without aesthetic preoccupations.
One walks through them with the police toward happiness.
Poetry, windows' spectacles, the secret of seamstresses.
There is no happiness greater than that of a well-dressed man.
Your heart is a horn prohibited by the traffic regulations.
The houses chew the tranquility of their oxen.
If you let it be known that you are a poet, you will go to the police station.
Wipe that enthusiasm from your eyes.

Automobiles rub against your hips turning your head. You must believe they are sinful women. In this way you will have your adventure and your smile for after dinner.

The flesh of the men you stumble on is calloused by offices.

Love is anywhere, but nowhere is it any different.

Workers walk by, their eyes resentful of the afternoon, the city, mankind.

Why would La Checa have shot you? You have hoarded nothing but your soul.

The city licks the night like a famished cat.

And you are a happy man, perhaps the only happy man.

You wear a shirt, and you have no great thoughts of any kind.

Right now I feel angry at those who accuse and those who console.

Spengler is an asthmatic uncle, and Pirandello is a stupid old man, almost one of his own characters.

But I mustn't get furious at trifles.

Thousands of the things men have done are worse than their cultures: Victor Hugo's novels, democracy, primary school, et cetera, et cetera, et cetera.

But men are bent on loving one another.

And, since they don't often succeed, they end up hating each other.

Because they do not want to believe that everything is irremediable.

I suspect the Greek city-state was a brothel to be approached with a revolver.

And the Greeks, in spite of their culture, were happy men.

I have not sinned much, but I already know about such things.

Bertoldo would say these things better, but Bertoldo would not ever say them. He doesn't dig very deep – and he's old, he wants peace, and he even supports the moderates.

The world is not exactly crazy, just overly decent. There is no
way to make it talk when it is drunk. And when it isn't, it ab-
hors drunkenness or loves its fellows.

But I honestly don't know what the world is or what mankind is.

I only know that I must be fair and honorable and love my fellow
man.

And I love the thousands of men within me that are born and die
each instant and do not live at all.

Behold my fellow men.

Justice is a few ugly statues in city squares.

I don't like any of them too much or too little – they are neither
hateful nor are they women.

I love the justice of women, without robes and without divinity.

As far as honor goes, I am not among the worst.

I eat my bread alone so as not to make my neighbor envious.

I was born in a city, and I don't know how to see the countryside.

I have been spared the sin of longing for it to be mine.

I do, on the other hand, desire heaven.

I am almost a virtuous man, almost a mystic.

I like the colors of the sky because it is certain they are not German inks.

I like to walk through the streets part-dog, part-machine, not at
all man.

I am not wholly convinced of my own humanity; I do not wish
to be like others. I do not want to be happy with permission
of the police.

Now there is a little sun in the streets.

I don't know who has taken it away, what evil man, leaving
stains on the ground like of a slaughtered animal.

A little crippled dog passes by: this is the only compassion, the
only charity, the only love of which I am capable.

Dogs do not have Lenin, and this guarantees them a human, but truthful life.

To walk through the streets like Pio Baroja's characters (all of them a bit doglike).

To chew on bones like Murger's poets, but serenely.

But men have an afterlife.

This is why they devote their lives to loving their fellow man.

They make money to kill useless time, empty time . . .

Diogenes is a myth – the humanization of dogs.

The longing great men have to be fully dogs. Little men want to be fully great men; millionaires, sometimes gods.

But these things should be said in a low voice – I am afraid of hearing myself.

I am not a great man – I am a common man who strives for great happiness.

But happiness is not enough to make one happy.

The world is too ugly, and there is no way to beautify it.

I can only imagine it as a city full of brothels and factories under the flapping of red flags.

My hands feel delicate.

What am I, what do I want? I am a man, and I do not want anything.

Or, perhaps, to be a man like bulls or others.

The rings under your eyes are not too big.

I want to be happy in a small way. With sweetness, with hope, with dissatisfactions, with limitations, with time, with perfection.

Now I can board a transatlantic liner. And during the crossing fish adventures as if they were fish.

But where would I go?

The world is insufficient for me.

It is too large, and I cannot shred it into little satisfactions as I would like.

Death is only a thought, nothing else, nothing else.

And I want it to be a long delight with its own end, its own quality.

The port, full of fog, is too romantic.

Cythera is a North American resort.

The flesh of Yankees is too fresh, almost cold, almost dead.

The panorama changes at every corner like a movie.

The final kiss already echoes through the shadows of a room full of burning cigarettes. But this is not the final scene. This is why the kiss echoes.

Nothing is enough for me, not even death; I want proportion, perfection, satisfaction, delight.

How have I ended up in this forsaken and smoky movie house?

The afternoon will have already ended in the city. And I still feel myself to be the afternoon.

I now remember perfectly my innocent years. And all bad thoughts are erased from my soul. I feel like a man who has never sinned.

I have no past, and an excess of future.

Let's go home . . .

B

Y THE TIME Ramon died, he had been left with only the vile and spent pleasure of looking under seats in public places: movie theater, streetcar, et cetera. One deep and empty day that rolled unconsciously from hour to hour, comatose like a cliff of stone upon stone, rock upon rock. The dirty cup of the sky was slowly filled with sugar, cold water, and lemon juice – a thirsty cloud licked its lips; Ramon died. Looking under seats . . . Ramon again became a compulsive smoker. Put out the cigarette, flick off the ash, trick the wind, stretch out an arm, all of which bawdily facilitated his enjoyment of taking his shoes by surprise when they were almost in their underwear, or of an after-dinner conversation, or of wasting away a Sunday. Sunday of shoes, shadows under the armchairs, a Saturday behind you, a dim light under the table . . . The shoes' after-dinner conversation, a short nap: a bootleg shakes the shoelaces loose; a toe cap yawns; the afternoon wrinkles its hide, tired of walking all morning; the right shoe turns on its side and snores. Shoes in their underwear; the uppers, made of yellow fabric, hang out, intimately, like a shirt. . . . Shoes, silent old people, in couples, disillusioned husbands, together at the heels, separate at the toes. The past married life unites them forever and distances them at the hour when they, he and she, would like to be twenty years old again, the right shoe and the left, the male and the female, the husband and the wife – to be twenty years old and marry badly or take a good lover. . . . The children's booties and slippers meet above, toe to toe, face to face, almost kissing, behind the folds of the nursemaid's apron. Shoes that are adolescent, elegant, languid, crazy, always misdirected, never decently parallel . . . shoes going through the bad years, the awkward age, weak lungs and robust tendencies . . . Old shoes, a soul alone in two bodies and not even loving each other . . . Ramon left the above verses typewritten on the index of a book with uncut pages I inherited from him.

Old shoes, one soul – a dirty layer of glue between the sole and insole – one soul in two bodies – two swollen and rheumatic bodies in a wrinkled hide – only one soul in two bodies . . . He and she don't want to face each other.

TERRIBLE days in which all women are one single woman wearing a nightgown. Terrible days of reading between the lines of Zamacois, terribly serious ... "No, don't give me Paul de Kock, Mister Kakison." Fifteen years old and wearing long pants ... ! No, life is a very serious thing – nothing less than a woman wearing a nightgown. Don't you understand me, Mister Kakison? It's possible you will never understand me. Admirable! ... What do you live on in London? That's not the point, Mister Kakison. Marina closes her window wearing her nightgown every night, but certainly that is not a sin. Why shouldn't she? Marina, hairy legs, an eight o'clock in the morning bather . . . To bathe at eight o'clock in the morning in the sea is to bathe in the cold, in the sky, in the hour. A shower of fog, a massage of chills, sponges of indecision, and the nearby barge – a large marine bird with black, drooping wings of folded nets, flies backwards. Hm . . . Mister Kakison, you must wash the stains of the night off your cinnamon-colored robe with benzine. Night in the robe of an English accountant of the firm Dasy & Bully . . . What do you say to that, Mister Kakison. "All right . . . ?" That is not an answer at this hour in this country. Say that I am right, and you will be well spoken. Yes, Mister Kakison, you will say something, the sanity of which you will never notice.

NIGHTTIME promenade. We have found a street hidden from the sky by dense, serious foliage. Here the sky does not exist; it has been rolled up like a rug, leaving barren the floorboards of space where the worlds – high society – take their strolls slowly, silently, fastidiously. Now I love you as I have never loved you: truly, painfully, I don't know how. . . . Walking through the street that returns our footsteps and our voices to us as in a cavern . . . A streetcar destroys a corner: an auger of light and sound. For a moment, we resound, we vibrate in this region of the night like all things: windows, windows, windows. . . . Now I can be a hero with a convex and bloody chest.

If I kidnapped you now, you would tear out locks of my hair and beg for mercy from the indifferent things. You will not do it. I shall not kidnap you, not for anything in the world. I need you in order to be at your side, longing to kidnap you. Woe to the one who realizes his desire! The sea sings in the distance like an approaching chorus in an opera. Suddenly it whispers in my ears like a glass of soda that is losing its gas. A piano is the entire night: its pain is antique, clichéd, a duet with four hands. . . . Now I will tell you how I feel:

"I love you because you love me. Your smallness orients my hope as I search for bliss. If you grew like the trees, I would not know what to desire. You are the measure of my pleasure. You are the measure of my desire. Behind all death is the joy of finding you in earthly paradises. Love, a little thing that never grows . . . If a star were to fall, you would catch it, and you would burn your hands. My love has not fallen from the sky, and that's why you do not catch it. You are dumb and pretty like all women. You laugh, and your laughter reconciles me with the night.

"Why do you not love me? You simply abandon me to the passing wind and the leaf that falls and the lamp that illuminates, as if by losing me you lose nothing. And my love at this hour is the only thing attentive to you. Now there is nothing you perturb except my love that follows you like your shadow, wanting to see your eyes. Love me, even though tomorrow, when you awake, you no longer remember me. Love me, the hour demands it of you! Woe to the one who disobeys time!"

Beyond the night, the dawning of the morning with its colors and its odors. Beyond the night, the birds' song matures in the future like the fruit of the trees. Beyond the night, your thoughts pick out realities to mix themselves up in. And my love follows you through the skyless night of the street, like the memory of a dog you once had that died.

A

T THE END of the very urban street, the country-side begins abruptly. From the huts, with their little patios and palm trees and campanilla bushes, the broom falls on the hillocks of spongy earth, over the adobe walls, on the monotonous blues of the sky. . . . Droves of asses carry adobe bricks all day long in a gray cloud of dust. Here, in patches on this hard and spongy ground, lie the city's future houses with their tarred roofs, delicate plaster window frames, living rooms with Victrolas and love secrets, perhaps even with their inhabitants—prudent mothers and modern girls, daredevil young men and industrious fathers. The face of a distant aunt can be divined in a clod of earth – the face of one of those aunts three times removed who comes for a visit to breath a little air, to drink a glass of cold water. A very old jacaranda – the retired municipal inspector of ornamentation – whiles away the hours, so many, of this first afternoon, making a few flowers of such expert perfection that, once finished, he tosses them away with the impassive nonchalance of a mandarin in his palace located in this sudden suburb. And on the horizon, a blinding smell of smoke erases the view of poplars and hillocks the pale, almost blue, color of granite. A dove passes low, carrying in its beak the bells of the parish church, and the bell is a piece of straw for its nest. An Indian girl pulls on the halter of an enormous mule; and she isn't even yet fifteen years old; and the mule grows stubborn and refuses to move; and the arc of the Indian girl's fragile body grows tenser and tenser; and the mule braces itself firmly with its front legs, and I want to kidnap this girl and run away with her on the mule to the mountains, so nearby, until its peaks scratch the skin off my nose, making me squint when I stare at them. I would descend, with the Indian girl in my arms and the mule between my legs, to a dark chasm full of cacti, with the somnambulistic certainty of a happy nightmare. . . . And the mule has pulled the halter out of the Indian girl's hands and now runs – wild, slouching, bent – in a loud and rapid trot along the road, hugging the wall, not knowing where to go. . . . And the halter it drags behind in the dust has the clean and perverse irony of a rat's tail. . . .

I HAVE received a letter from Catita. She says nothing in it except that she would like to see me with a sad face. It is a long letter, tremulous, in which a nubile girl pulls love by the ears with those sure, those slow, those surgical fingers women use for their tortures from the age of fifteen until they deliver their first child. . . . There are women who never conceive, and it is they whom Death fears most, for in order to carry them to the other world, he must wage a fierce battle during which his skeleton is sure to get a severe scratching: spinsters die heroically.

Catita's letter smells of spinsterhood – of incense, dried flowers, soap, plaster, medicine, milk. Emblematic spinsterhood with tortoiseshell glasses and a stiff index finger. A blue bun gives the final touch to the inevitably partial countenance. A skirt licks the austere perfume exuded by the silk lace of the blouse. And a blouse of poetic fabrics – a robe of madapollam. And moreover, an indispensable detail, a long face whose features – both hard and weak, rough and useless – create the face out of buckram folds. Perhaps a polly that knows the litany of Loreto . . . Perhaps the portrait of an unlikely suitor . . . Perhaps an obsession to know everything . . . Perhaps a virtue crowned with thorns . . . But Catita is not even fifteen years old yet. The truth is, there is no reason her fingers should know how to pull on ears. Who knows if some boy, mad with love, doesn't already want to marry her? Catita, taster of young boys, a bad woman who already has the hands of a spinster before the age of fifteen . . . English spinster, expert in explosives, propaganda department; a strange, short man; dry, veined hands . . . Is that how you'd like to be, Catita? What should I do with your letter? At this hour it is the impossible of all impossibilities for me to be sad. I am happy at this hour – it's a habit of mine. A fishing boat off the coast of Miraflores waves with its white handkerchief of a sail – so useless in this still, pretty atmosphere, as if painted by a second-rate artist. This greeting is a greeting to nobody, and that happiness, a happiness of nonsense, of smallness, of regress, of humility . . . My cigarette draws admirably, and it is the rejoicing of a youthful fire with blue and minuscule rings and balls; and it is the rural peace of the smell of burnt brambles. You see, Catita? You don't see anything because you are not with me on the promenade above the sea; but I swear to you it is just as I say. In the afternoon, facing the sea, my soul becomes good, small, silly, humane, and is gladdened by the fishing boats that unfurl their joke of a sail, and by the burning ember of the cigarette – a red-haired child who loses his head in a blue toy shop.

And high-flying bulls – black flies in the sky's mug of watery milk – make me want to shoo them away with my hands. When I was five years old and didn't want to drink my milk, I would drown in it flies that I trapped with a spoon – a net compressed by the light until it hardened – and the flies in the milk turned into propellers. And now, suddenly, I feel like a naughty child, and I refuse to drink the glass of milk of the sky because it has no sugar in it. And Mother Totuca, sweet ebony Buddha, might come along with the sugar bowl painted with a boy monkey dressed as a pirate and a girl monkey dressed as a Dutch girl, together making reverential gestures over the blue band stretching around the Buddha's belly. . . . Perhaps your star would become sweeter if I sweetened the sky with sugar – your star: so bitter; your star: a spinster who falls in love with impossible comets; your star: that leads you down the wrong path of love. Did you hear, Catita? I cannot get sad at this hour – at this hour – the only one of the day in which I am happy, unconscious, like a child; my hour of foolishness; my hour, Catita. You tasted Ramon, and he did not taste bad to you. Well, okay, so I will be Ramon. I will take upon myself his duty of kissing you on your wrists and looking at you with foolish eyes – worthy of all of Ramon's sayings. Foolish and large-winged duty accepted at an insular, celestial, windy, open, desolate hour. I will be Ramon for one month, two months, for however long you can love Ramon. But no: Ramon is dead, and Ramon never wore a sad face and, above all, you have already tasted Ramon. Yes, Catita, it's true, but I am not a sad man. As I am at this hour – foolish and happy – so I am most of the day. I am a cheerful boy. I was born with a happy mouth. My life is a mouth that speaks, that eats, and that smiles. I don't believe in astrology. I accept that there are sad stars and happy stars. I even assert that sad stars are an excellent motive for writing sonnets with lines of fourteen syllables. But I do not believe our lives have any relationship whatsoever with the stars. Oh, Catita! Life is not a river that flows: life is a puddle that stagnates. During the day, the same trees, the same sky, the same day is reflected in it. At night – always the same stars, the same moon, the same night. Sometimes an unknown face – a boy, a poet, a woman – is reflected in it – the older the puddle, the murkier – and then the face disappears because a countenance will not eternally contemplate itself in the puddle. And the countenance does contemplate itself. And the puddle is barely a turbid and interceding mirror. And an old man is a puddle in which no young girl would look at herself. Because one's own life is a puddle, but the lives of others are faces that come to look at themselves in it. Yes, Catita. But some lives are not puddles, but rather a lake, a sea, an ocean wherein only the sky and the mountains, the clouds, the great ships can be seen. Thus the life of Walt Whitman – a Yankee who was half-crazy and therefore an excellent poet – was an ocean full of trans-atlantic liners; Napoleon's, on the other hand, was an ocean full of warships and cetaceans. Saint Francis' was a trough from which a donkey with a dove perched on its forehead drank. Phillip II's: a dead sea with a very sad countenance and sinister legends. Puccini's: an alpine lake, white with canoes from the Cook Travel Agency. Bolivar's: a canal, dangerous with reefs and frightening with floating barrels. Your life: a washbasin in which one soaks an armful of broom that has the color and smell of sulphur. Thus is the soul, Catita – either enemy waters or foolish waters – lake, sea, swamp, washbasin full of water. But never a flow with a current and a bed. My life is a hole dug in the sands of a beach by the hands of a truant child – a malignant and tiny hole that distorts the reflection of gentlemen who scold truant children, the image of respectable gentlemen who come to the beach and infest the sea air – so clean, so brilliant – with their terrible smells of the office. Such is my life, Catita – a little puddle on a beach – so now you see why I cannot get sad. The high tide undoes me, but another truant child digs me again at the other end of the beach, and I cease to exist for a few days, during which time I learn, always anew, the joy of not existing and that of resuscitating. And I am the truant child who digs his life in the sands of the beach. And I know the insanity of setting life up against destiny, because destiny is nothing more than the desire we feel alternately to die and to resuscitate. For me the horror of death is nothing more than the certainty of not being able to resuscitate ever again, that eternal boredom of being dead. Oh Catita, don't read sad books, and don't read the happy ones either! There is no happiness greater than being a little hole full of sea water on a beach, a hole that is destroyed by the high tide, a little hole full of sea water in which floats a paper boat. To live is nothing more than to be a truant child who makes and un-makes his life in the sands of the beach, and there is no pain greater than being a hole full of seawater on a beach that is bored of being that, or of being someone who is too easily undone. Catita, don't read destiny in the stars. They know as little about it as you do. Sometimes the puddle of my life coincides with the fall of one of them, and I have had more than one of them in my drop of water. Catita, the stars know nothing about issues that concern girls. They themselves are perhaps nothing more than girls with boyfriends, with mothers, and with spiritual ad-dresses. What you decipher in them is nothing more than your own concerns, your own joys, your own sadnesses. Moreover, stars have a much too provincial beauty, I don't know . . . too naive, too truthful. . . . The poor things imitate your way of viewing things. Your star is nothing more, no doubt, than a star that views things as you do, and its flickering is nothing more than fatigue at having to look in a way that has nothing to do with its feelings. Catita . . . Catita, why does your destiny have to be in the sky? Your destiny is here on Earth, and I have it in my hands, and I feel a terrible desire to throw it into the sea, over the railing. But no. What would you be without your destiny? Your destiny perhaps is to be a puddle on an ocean beach, a puddle full of seawater, but a puddle in which there is, instead of a paper boat, a little fish that raises a fat and brutish wave.

S ERGIO ... He had a name that did not suit him ... a serene and chaste name, with a touch of the steppe, of fatality, and of popishness. He was a boy with piggish eyes who sometimes, while he was doing some mischief, had a small, sharp, black, apish glint in them. All of him was in his skin: such coldness, such nuance, such smoothness, and an amber light. He was also in his head that was crowned with a mop of stiff, curly, chestnut hair over a bald forehead. I can only remember him as a man who passes quickly through a crowded, squat, fenced-off street, hiding his face in his hurry. He was also in the sound of his heels as he walked, the colorless dry sound of beaten wood.

Sergio was in his whole figure. It was impossible to know anything else about him: Sergio lied like nobody else, with his entire soul, beyond the truth and all likelihood, beyond. . . . And so it was, always. One day, Sergio became a priest. And nothing was ever heard from him again. Eugenio D'Ors, the distinguished Dominican philosopher, can write his life story — Sergio's and his own — with the sacred hope of finding out for a certainty why a boy with the eyes of a pig who lied like nobody else became a priest. And D'Ors could even recount his death to us in advance — Sergio's: under a crucifix as large and cruel as death itself, hanging from a word made simple by solitude, by a whole morning spent in his treacherous cell. And he could add great subtleties to the simplicity of the death of a priest with a scraggly beard that had once been young and highly sexual. Oh, what a marvelous book Eugenio D'Ors could write about Sergio's life and death! How fitting, to a stupid and unmotivated life, is the philosophy — so down to earth, so good-looking, so nurturing, so charming, so ingenuous, so damn Catalonian — of this Commentator! I seem to be reading: ". . . and so . . . But let us examine, Commentator, and may we not be carried away by love. . . . Measure . . . Compare . . . " But, I don't know why, once in a while I believe that Sergio never died; that, at the hour of his death, he pretended to be dead; that he let himself be buried and then unburied himself two days later and returned to Lima to escape from the monastery and begin a new life. If only this were so . . . But then Eugenio D'Ors' book could not be written, and I would never know anything about Sergio.

H

E GRABBED one of her hands. She inserted one of her fat legs, either one, perhaps someone else's, under his right leg that was bent back as if ready to kick. His countenance burned red like a traffic light or the sign of a late-night pharmacy. Suddenly it turned, and there appeared another face, identical to the first, only yellow. This was the sign of detention. She remained impassive like a prostitute. She smiled candidly, dug her leg in further, and bit her lower lip without blinking. Ramon grew thinner. She grew fatter. Ramon was an animal that began to have ideas. She was a woman who began to become a beast. Suddenly the sun was lit by a terrible, rose-colored warning light. The night train passed with a deafening roar. She and Ramon boarded the last car. The sad and dark freight car.

S H E W A S a fierce taster of boys. All of us were to roll our heads over her firm, round little bosom. In this way, from this inevitable love, we created eras: "When I courted Catita . . . " But it was Catita who courted us. When we looked at her, she winked and didn't notice. Her eyes: round like the rest of her . . . And her name did not name her well. The *i* in the penultimate syllable made her long, dreary, distant: she who was close, round, happy. And, above all, a sucker for love. Catalina is a Gothic name; it makes one think of gray ogives at twilight, of bronze, moss-covered fountains, of dwarfed, chaotic villages, of bulky chastity belts. . . . And Catita was a blond window at noon; a clean, modern, white cement fountain; a large, tattered sunshade for the beach; a schoolgirl's crazy hair ribbon. . . . Lala, such is her name. But Lala was a quick and cautious girl. Lala, Lala, Lala . . . Soft heart and doll eyes and a laughing face. Ramon threw himself into Catita like a swimmer into the sea – from head to foot, hands first, then the head, and finally the feet: flexed and worn down at the heels. On the staff of the month of January – still greased with dirty, cold clouds – Ramon hung in the sky – in the air, in the middle, balanced, in his bathing suit, at the very top, with a hundred trembling boys behind him, rushing him – over Catita, over the sea. Ramon had a bad fall – a belly flop that splashed all of us, unprepared observers. Catita, a sea to bathe in at twelve o'clock noon with the stupefying sun on your head, a dry butterfly, jaundiced brambles, or a yellow bathing cap. Catita, a sea with waves because there are no old ladies, because there are boys. . . . Catita, round sea protected by a semicircular pier, emblazoned with cities . . . Catita, subtle boundary between the high and the low tides . . . Catita, sea submissive to the moon and the bathers . . . Catita, sea with lights, seashells, with little potbellied boats, sea, sea, sea . . . Oh, love that also had no old ladies, no straw sunshades, no advice, no genuflections . . . Catita, love, with fat and gentle hope, love that rises and falls with the moon, round love, close love, love in which to sink oneself, to snorkel in with open eyes, love, love, love . . . Catita, sea of love, love of sea. Catita, anything and nothing . . . Catita – appearing in all the vowels, whole, complete, in body and soul – in the *a* and disappearing little by little, feature by feature, in the others; in the *e:* tender and foolish; in the *i:* skinny and ugly; in the *o:* almost her, but not quite . . . Catita is honest and pretty; in the *u:* albino and cretino . . . Catita, like some consonants, so much like the *b,* in her hands; the *n,* in her eyes; the *r,* in her walk; the *ñ,* in her personality; the *k,* in her character; the *s,* in her bad memory; the *z,* in her good faith . . . Catita, a round field in the sea, a round kiss in love . . . Catita, sound, symbol . . . Catita, any old thing and exactly the opposite . . . Catita, in the end, a pretty girl, sincere, alive, flirtatious as only she can be . . . To trap her was as impossible as stopping up with the tip of the index finger the flow of water from the mouth of a large spigot; flesh firm under the pressure of a touch, flesh that escaped through the cracks in the nail, through the lines on the skin; that jumped out at us; that, if deposited in a receptacle, quietly, would only be dense light, water to drink and in which to launch paper boats. Water, water, water . . . And at the end of it all, a pretty, lovesick girl, taster of boys, Catita . . .

ON THE rooftop, the unique and multiple air, wrapped entirely around itself, rolling invisibly in currents like Bulgarian milk in bacillus culture; on the rooftop, in the air, dense with the sun's rubber bands, with colorless mucilages of humidity; on the rooftop: the lady's underwear. It is here in the humid regions of the air where the blue of the sky is bluer, and when an unnameable bird passes behind this region it grows and grows as if seen through the eye of a needle. It is a window in a one-story house – a dreamy vision of the still, dirty, insane room, of crystals bleached by the afternoon's oblique reflection; the gentleman's jacket with its silver chain and its watch hidden in the pocket. Through the same window appear – instead of the gentleman's flesh supported by the gentleman's clavicle – two naked spheres: the top of the back of the Viennese chair. Old bones, already the appalling color of skeletons exhumed long years after burial . . . With my back to the sun, I open with the shadow of my head a dark hole in the light of the crystal. There they are, the jacket and the chair, not nightmarish horrors, but rather humane, familiar, spontaneous, frank, at home. The potbellied gentleman. His cashmere jacket sags at the bottom and nags the canework to fatten up, set it straight, fill it out. . . . The canework: skinny, pious, a spinster. All the buttons on the jacket are closed except for the last one whose corresponding buttonhole has the rounded and empty mischievousness of an old man's eye; a veracious, sexual eye, in the open air like the lady's underwear on the rooftop. . . . The jacket might be a sixty-year-old drunkard, a cynic, a womanizer, an oaf – if it had a nose, it would be red, oily, hairy, covered with pimples. In a silence that sounds abrupt, sudden, violent, we might believe we hear the ticktock of the clock, the jacket's impious and stubborn heart. The chain is arched and expresses nothing – so, nearly horizontal, relaxed, it is the jacket's conscience. The canework sits in the wooden chair with the most austere decency, as if she were in church or at a conference on domestic hygiene; the torso and thighs at right angles. She has eliminated her belly, her breasts, her legs, out of a sense of modesty; her arms, we know not why; her face, for the sake of decency. She has avoided sinning by removing one dimension from herself. That is why we imagine the canework – two ascetic, livid balls – with a curl of hair on her forehead to banish bad thoughts; with only one gray hair in her black lacquer bun to remind her of death when she looks at herself in the mirror; with a mole on the tip of her nose, we don't know why; with a short Latin prayer on her lips to avoid useless words. The day cackles. A hen cackles like the day – secretive, implacable, obvious, discontinuous, vast. A frond rubs against a house: the chaste swallows protest. Above, the cirrous sky. Below is the street extensively, energetically stained with light and shadow as if with soot and chalk. The gentleman's jacket belches, swells, and finally, belches. With their brooms, sharp and straight like paintbrushes, the street sweepers make drawings along the tree-lined streets. The street sweepers have the hair of aesthetes, the eyes of drug addicts, the silence of literary men. There are no shadows. Yes, there is one shadow: an emanation of light in vain spreads through the street that grows longer and longer in order to cancel it out. Here the shade is not the negation of the light. Here the shade is ink; it covers things with an imperceptible dimension of thickness; it gives color. The light is a white floury dust that the wind disperses and carries far away. A ragged youngster inserts a rope into naked spools of thread. I insert wooden adjectives into the thick, rugged rope of an idea. At the end of the street, blocking it, a blue wall grows pale until it turns into the sky itself. This city is definitely not a village. The donkeys devoutly respect the sidewalks. Donkeys that only bray in the neighborhood at determined hours . . . Donkeys that do the unmentionable behind a tree or a post without lifting a leg . . . Donkeys that do not dare graze on the grassy patches but stick close to the cement edge of the gutters . . . Donkeys that sing like the roosters when the roosters oversleep . . . Donkeys that, on the side of the street with a sidewalk, graze on the low, cartwright-beheading branches of the trees . . . Oh these donkeys – the only remaining villagers in the city – have become municipalized, bureaucratized, humanized . . . ! Donkeys want their commendations recognized in order to obtain their election rights: to elect and be elected. . . . Through the smells of kitchen, of frying oil, a world enclosed within this world is revealed to me: the world of the barnyard. The roosters also become human, though not in a sane, patriotic, sensible way like the donkeys, but rather in a strange, impertinent, exotic way. Not turning into men, but rather Englishmen. Those roosters, eccentric gringos who wear Scottish wool, who engage in a foolish sport like worm-hunting, play soccer with miserly bones and cobs of corn, constantly shiver from the cold, rise at dawn, and do not understand females. Soon they will smoke pipes, read magazines, play polo – instant gentlemen – and take pleasure trips to Southampton on a P.S.N.C. ship. Hens are good mothers who still make an effort to please their husbands. Moral standards in the barnyard are falling. If it weren't for the solid good faith and austere habits of the ducks . . . If it weren't for the antimilitaristic and clerical traditionalism of the turkeys – scanty hygiene, bad smells, preterition, chess matches, runny noses, great-great-grandfathers who were Counts, mortgages . . . Ducks don't know about these things – the husband, the shop, the ladies, the house and the children; one must be well fed, virtuous, and save for old age.

The ducks would disapprove of Nansen's trip to the South Pole. Ducks – I don't know why – always seem to be fighting with some aunt over a damned inheritance. We don't know if the ducks descend from immigrants from the South or from some imaginary French consul, married to a Paraguayan woman and settled in Lima, where he died in 1832 or 1905. Rabbits have long ears, as we all know, but they are good fellows. Very little is known about them: they are, it is true, always well dressed, but they live in caves. One additional fact: they read Pitigrilli. We might say they are middle-class, meddlesome, busybodies, know-it-alls, with bastards in their family history. . . . Soon they will acquire a late-model Ford limousine and a second-hand pianola. The girls are lovely. There will be weekly receptions. Where does the money come from? From nothing honorable, undoubtedly. Their fortune was gotten in a bad way, according to *vox populi*. The rabbits' friendship is very sought after by everyone. But if the rabbits are not decent people, absolutely decent, this friendship will be revoked. Rabbits wink their alcoholic eyes, vermilion from the sun, and hide their Semitic mouths. The geese are wealthy country gentlemen, always just passing through. They have a suspicious look in their eyes; their accent: from the mountains; their bellies: full; their families: back at the hacienda. . . . They never give alms. He and she . . . Exemplary spouses. Both of them, obese. Sometimes a goat — bad head, bad head, bad head . . . swerves like a sleepwalker when walking. He is photophobic, like a good night bird. His age? . . . Doesn't have one. Twenty years old . . . Fifty years old . . . These madcaps don't have an age, but rather a character; not a personality, rather a vice . . . or many vices. A face between that of Mephistopheles and Uncle Sam. He could have had a job in the government, but he doesn't, the devil of a goat. He is a cuckold without even being married. He spouts bitter philosophies about matrimony. There is nothing as wonderful as having no commitments. Long live idleness, the good life! . . . The goat gets bored; the goat gets bored; the goat gets bored . . . Guinea pigs, all of them, male and female, are female. They are the servants of the turkey and the turkey hen. Their faces are small and swarthy, their eyes are small and shiny, their stature is small and bent, their step is small and lively. They are all that remain from Castile's colonial slave trade. The young turkeys call them mommies. The horses prepare the old Creole dishes; they have milked the turkey mother, dehorned the turkey father, they know all the family secrets, are disdainful of the ducks, and never go out because they don't have enough money to buy a new blanket. They look like little old half-breed ladies:

spouting proverbs, devout, ill-tempered, gossip-mongers. The pigeons are the scandal of the barnyard. They speak French, are indecorously sentimental, go everywhere alone, and are more than a little *cocotte*. Their Yankee partiality for balladeers make them faint on the tenth floor, prompting the male pigeons to dress all in white and neglect their children.

The countryside, bloody with green blood. The cheeks and lips of some of the figurines' fancies are also green. The field's fat face has one gray eye of a puddle that laughs like an idiot. The other eye – the right one – is the sun, in the flesh and without a pupil. This landscape has spent five months in a mental hospital jumping up and down on one foot and tearing itself to pieces with ten clawed, black fingers. This landscape, hysterical masochist, with a history of syphilis . . . This battered, rugged landscape . . . This landscape: one-eyed and sexless . . . In its naked belly, the ecchymosis of fallow lands. On its gray forehead, the boils of a clearing. On its chest, like a scapular, a strange fetus, the obsession of a church. The rain quiets the crazed landscape. Its visions are now tame, sane, almost true – the vaccinated, treacherous afternoon is beaten on its opaque flanks, its rough haunches, with the heavy trail of the sun's rays: straight, yellow. And a cow, realer than everything, behind a mud wall, weaves moos through the tattered grass.

I DREAM of an iconography of Ramon that would allow me to remember him, so plastic, so special, plastically, spatially. All that remains for me of Ramon is the serious bitterness of having known him, his permission to leaf through his intimate diary in Señorita Muler's silly little alcove, a trail of cigarette butts along the city's longest street, and a way of thinking and seeing that makes it possible for me to live in the midst of this amorphous group of houses, encaustic streets, naive trees, this somewhat pesty, somewhat lagunalike sea, on this plane that suddenly acquires three dimensions and ten thousand inhabitants. Oh, the sea! Only the sea has not ceased to be those long black waves, pencil lines meticulously equidistant from the thousands of curves along the beach. The mountains cannot be seen from the side, only from above, the high mountains in contoured lines; the hills cut with an axe. Obsessive precision with canvases and projections, scales and numbers. May God bless Ramon, that crazy guy who taught me how to see the water in the sea, the leaves on the trees, the houses on the streets, the sex of women. Around here Ramon has become lines, lights, secrets, face, ornaments, details, grass fibers, bells. . . . No, no. An iconography, an album in black and sepia through whose pages he would pass, with his melancholy mouth, his illusive glasses, and his terrible insignificance, a road anywhere. Or standing in front of rusty old sheds, or under green street lamps, or against yellow twilights. Or judiciously sitting on a parochial school bench or on the drunken benches along the promenade, or on the slippery chairs of the electric streetcar. Or chasing girls made of gelatin and organdy, or fat shadows, or illuminated windows, or unsociable dogs. With one leg outstretched or with both legs stiff and together. Inapprehensible, but indubitable, unmistakable. On difficult afternoons of light and tedium, I might open the album and ask Ramon: "What should I do now, my friend?" And he might answer as he used to during the happy days of his life in the mountains: "Whatever you want." And I would do what I wanted: walk through the streets that smell, at that hour, of honey and kitchen mops. Under the convex sky – a lemon peel turned inside out – the sounds grow until they become visible, the trees sharpen their branches *à la cypress,* and an old man walking by pounding the cobblestones with his iron stick drags his shapeless shadow along the ground like a cloak. An automobile drives at seventy kilometers per hour – a speed definitely prohibited – through a street traversed only by donkeys loaded with sandbags. The mayor is by now just barely that gentleman with a pointed beard whom everyone should obey. Yesterday, the sun rose ten minutes after it should have risen. Something more: it penetrated the only place it should not have penetrated: between the ears of the only baker's ass we have left in the city. The cold has long and white muscles like one of those rachitic athletes who sometimes carry off the trophy at the championship games, runts one meter high and with the hands of a typist. The air rubs the sky and scratches it the way a diamond scratches a crystal. I do whatever I want. A dove has carried away my last good thought. Now I am as I truly am: clean, Asiatic, refined, bad. Now I have a round rubber neck. Now I jump over an old woman who examines her shoe on the street, poor old blind woman. Ramon loved the cooks who gave themselves to their bosses' sons in the barnyard, in the haystacks and brick piles where the birds brood. The bells of Saint Francis hum a light melody – the prior doesn't hear them. A section of the sky collapses over a corner of the sea, on this side of the island. A closed, double window – the gesture of a decent house, the wink of a pharmacist's spectacles. There will appear, at night, when nothing can be seen, a face that is pretty, pretty, pretty . . .

T HE PAVING stones – undergoing noontime helio-
therapy, recumbent, facing the sun. In the corridor of the street
– the windows of air have been opened – the policeman is the
doctor who observes, who observes. . . . Among the paving
stones there is only one clinically interesting case – a triangular
stone on the corner, at the intersection of two sidewalks (Miss
C. V., twenty-three years old, daughter of consumptive parents.
Miss C. V. swallows. Miss C. V. has her eyes closed. Miss C. V.
dies. Cancer of the uterus? . . . The name of the disease is unknown. Miss C. V. is a very interesting case.) The rest of the
stones have -algas, -itis, -osis, horribly general – married and
widowed women who, in order to prolong the hour, prolong

their convalescence. When it is impossible to have a lover because you are sixty years old, the best thing to do is lie in the sun with your eyes closed and forget your husband, dead or alive. These sexual hours of dinner and digestion . . . A good time of day at the sanatoriums. The front row, the one in the shade, is a row of sick individuals of the masculine sex, an allusive and tragic masculine sex. In their heads, dark and painful, pounds the fever of business. Through their veins and arteries, wagon carts come and go. In their ears, telephones ring. The smell of sickness, the smell of the taste of bile, become the smells of the office – the smell of cedar and reams of paper. A turkey buzzard, with the bent, sallow fortitude of a diabetic Norseman, leaves for a station in the highlands of the Swiss sky that has already turned on its ices, its snows, its hotels for the tourists . . . – manager of an oil company, fifteen years of equatorial, Venezuelan, xenophobic sunshine. . . . Bible readings, silent black beer, Swedish exercise, prodigiously not adjusting, the frugal, austere pleasures of a preseptentrional immigrant to this America: luminous, caliginous, brutish, hard, mineral, Miocenic, maritime . . . The paving stones are stones carved with a hammer. The sun kills them, but they do not complain. I don't know why they are here, suffering without paying. Twenty little breedless, tailless dogs (large ears; the hanging ones are of sheepskin; the erect ones of felt) that range in color from the waxen hue of fresh straw to the bluing on steel, rush along behind one large purebred dog with a tail and a mundane, uncouth, opulent face. . . . The dogs glide along on short, agile limbs. The sun turns all the dogs into gold ingots. Hungering after the great female . . . The Social revolution . . . Princess Alexandra Canoff, you who run along this street, almost as solitary and sunny as Tsarkoieselo, your Parisian follies are now over. Freud does not include those of Caron, or those of Coty in his coprolitic smells

. . . This bitch smells like *Christmas Eve,* like *The Nights of Siam,* like I don't know what night, just so long as you do not say the afternoon. What a good idea it is to give the name of night to perfumes. All perfumes are nocturnal. Sometimes I think that flowers exist only to temper the emotions of the day. The very same sun that is just barely a jovial and idle Barranco sun shining in these rose gardens, becomes Libyan, Saharan in the desert; this matchmaking sun, without a family, a bachelor, a gossip-monger from five continents; pretender; this gallant sun that of-fers his arm to abandoned aunties on promenades. . . . Flowers absorb light and heat, releasing carbonic gas during absorption. At night, wherever there is a flower, there is also a gnomic light with a tender halo of heat enclosed within the *cocotte* shade of each corolla. The sea is also the outskirts of the city. Now the sea is a mirror that reflects the sky, a thick and enormous looking glass quicksilvered with mullets and corbinas. The sea is green because the sky is green. The sky, immense face, green and fea-tureless . . . The sea can be a picturesque sea, naive, full of fish. But now it is a mirror. The sky can be a field for farming or live-stock. But it isn't; now it is a face that looks at itself in the mirror of the sea. A heartsick torch in a street that could have been and wasn't . . . ; earthward, a stump of a sidewalk, and that spirit of foolish desire common to all streets. A rooster turns to me with a cruel, mechanical gesture, his bald head, his sharp, ivory profile, his carmine, British ears. The sea hoists tar-covered birds and bundles of waves with the crane of the rusty island. The opaque marine solarium – sun glares rusted by water – trickle of oil at a given moment, suddenly, a large splash of mercury that drowns, that sinks . . . A mine from the great war, a broken egg from Moeaee . . . I don't know which unnoticeable slope in the streets always takes me to the outskirts of town. The sea is the outskirts as well.

THE AFTERNOON arises from this slow-moving, dapple-gray mule with a long stride. From her emanates – in waves that make visible the light of three o'clock postmeridian and reveal the canvas of the atmosphere – the movie screen, a round one that does not need darkness; from her all things emanate. At the end of each bundle of rays: a house, a tree, a lamp, myself. This mule is creating us as it imagines us. Through her I feel the solidarity of my origins with the animate and the inanimate. We are all images conceived during a calm and supple trot, images that become foliated, plastered, and fenestrated, or are clothed in drill, or topped with a glass helmet. Cosmic logic divides us into undefined species of only one kind . . . a window and I . . . a sea gull and I . . . With each step the mule takes – a step that is duplex, rotund, eternally inalterable, predetermined by a divine genius – my being trembles at unknowable destiny. At this moment the mule has never existed. The mule has been annulled around a corner. Now the afternoon is itself – atheistic, autogenetic, romantic, liberal, desolate. These famished dogs – mute scavengers with protruding backbones, sagging hides, and arched bodies – look like cats, street cats with realistic, socialistic, enlightened, herbivorous eyes. A gust of wind unfurls a Chinese flag at a towering height, as if it were a parchment, from left to right – the flag veils precisely that rectangle of the sky where the sun is. The afternoon grows black, and night becomes. The posts, along these streets of low and nitrous walls, have the rather violent appearance of pedestrians. The day, with its invariable rainy mood, holds them for its fourteen hours at the edge of the sidewalk. Soon after nightfall, the posts begin to walk. Summer nights: flowing like black beer with gray, star-studded foam . . . The posts have worked very hard, they grew tired, were widowed, the only son went to Guatemala . . . By now their arms are falling off from just plain old age. And if their backs are not bent, it is only because their bones are made of wood. Aged electricians with hands dried and corroded by the gutta-percha and balata gum, by leaking batteries, and greasy tools . . . They are retired, and have acquired, along with the pleasure of a full salary and the right to frolic, the lines of certain ex-public officials who have fallen out of favor with the present government, survivors of distant battles, eccentric old uncles who collect herbs and postage stamps. . . . Between one post and the next there is a distance of twenty-five meters that never decreases or increases – the posts neither love nor hate one another . . . misanthropy, misogyny, at the most a grumble of irritation or a greeting from one to the other, and this only because they can't not do so. . . . At night the posts go for walks. On a street quite far away, I have recognized a post that spends the whole day at the door of my house holding his hat, stiff and thoughtful, as if suffering quietly from a pain in the kidneys or doing arithmetic in its head. The posts never unite. The distances during these strange walks remain constant: they are, as if tied with a rope around their waists: mountain climbers on the mountain of their lives at twenty-five degrees below zero. We attribute to them the reckless daring of men without families or trite pleasures – a Count Godeneau-Platana, pederast and Egyptologist; another Prince Giustati, Castilian and aesthete; a Mexican millionaire suddenly impoverished by a revolution . . . The following morning (mornings always follow) the posts return to their assigned places. And there they are while fourteen gyrating hours mutate the color of the air – long, skinny, erect, rigid, wondering whether or not it will rain. One post is called Julian because he lets his beard grow. . . . the beard: paper streamers from the Carnival of 1912. Another post is called Matias, because that is his name. A poor asthmatic post on Mott Street dreams of buying an overcoat made of French fabric. There are posts that cater to dogs. There are posts that are friends of beggars. There are European posts with the green eyes of crystal insulation. There are street-lamp posts. There are telephone posts.

AN ICE CREAM vendor's trumpet drew attention to a nocturnal howling of dogs, symphony of tin and moon, torn from the beginning, the tear exposing black, canine palates bristling with papillas as hard as callouses. If their singing could be musically annotated, it would have to be done on a temperature scale, on graph paper, with a dotted line, with uneven numbers. Musical skeleton. Forty-two degrees Fahrenheit, mortal fever. A spring of light and dust rise to the sun from a nearby field surrounded by thick adobe walls. A rising, trailing wind lifts the spring and contracts it without bending it. Hidden, childish, imprisoned . . . Over the mud entablature, behind, ill-

comet, the upper funnel broken along the wind's axis, tilt of an elliptic circumference, clear, closed curve. At night this street will be a different street. We shall walk by here without knowing where we are going. At noon, footsteps make no sound. The shadow follows alongside, dwarfed, shapeless, the silhouette of an unkempt gangster feigning an attack. Silence closes its parentheses at each window. Ramon, shaving soap, green blanket, holy palm at the head of his bed – and the window, barely opened onto the heat of a yellow sky; oh, second floors in a low town! – an oozing eucalyptus tree that drops round moments into the painted gutter, delicate balls of scorched paper, burned and rolled-up leaves – folk medicines, ancient recipes, rest, rest . . . Sweaty, dark-skinned girl, a mere gesture suddenly makes you so ugly, so pretty if you stand under the light at the edge of the pavement, breath of summer, afternoon nap dreams. . . . Your step falls into rhythm with mine. I don't know what to say to you. A sudden gust of cold wind changes our lives. You disappear from my consciousness every instant, and when you return, you are warm, like the hat or the book we leave in the bright sun when we escape to the shade. The wide street opens our eyes, violently, until it hurts and blinds us. The whole town drags itself along . . . posts, trees, people, streets . . . along the banks of this stream of freshness and sea breezes. In the oven of sun, the houses made of bread dough bake and get burned on the bottom. You no longer walk by my side. A sexton extinguished the sun with a willow branch. And six steel bells – *Ite missa est* – spoke simply, ritualistically, mechanically. The sultriness is over, as is our sitting still, the tedium of being indoors, and the inevitable shadow of this four-hour mass.

MARTÍN ADÁN was born in Peru in 1908. In Lima, where his iconoclastic and solitary life represents his total rejection of the oligarchic circles into which he was born, he became a legend in his own time. Known primarily as a poet, Adán twice won the National Prize for Poetry, and was a member of the Peruvian Chapter of the Academy of the Spanish Language.

KATHERINE SILVER has also translated the work of Carlos Fuentes, Antonio Skarmeta, José Emilio Pacheco, and Elena Poniatowska. She lives in Oakland, California.

This book was designed by Tree Swenson.

It is set in Galliard type by The Typeworks and

manufactured by Edwards Brothers on acid-free paper.